The Storm

and Other Erotica

ALSO BY RÉGINE DEFORGES:

La Bicyclette Bleue

(The Devil Laughs Again)

The Storm

and Other Erotica

R é g i n e   D e f o r g e s

Translated from the French by Rosette Lamont

Grove Press
New York

Published simultaneously in Canada
Printed in the United States of America

FIRST AMERICAN EDITION

Library of Congress Cataloging-in-Publication Data
Deforges, Régine.
   [Orage. English]
   The storm : and, Other erotica / Régine Deforges.
      p.   cm.
   ISBN 0-8021-3632-X
   1. Deforges, Régine—Translations into English.   2. Erotic
stories, French—Translations into English.   I. Deforges, Régine.
Contes pervers. English.   II. Title.   III. Title: Storm ; and,
Other erotica.   IV. Title: Other erotica.
PQ2664.E442A2   1999
843'.914—dc21   99-19684
                                                                      CIP

Design by Laura Hammond Hough

Grove Press
841 Broadway
New York, NY 10003

99 00 01 02   10 9 8 7 6 5 4 3 2 1

Contents

The Storm

and Other Erotica

The Storm

TO PIERRE

m I right?

After hesitating for many years, I decided that these pages, written some twenty years ago by a very young woman in love, should be published. Despite their obscene character, and almost unbearable scenes, I judged that this raw text was one of the most beautiful love stories I have ever encountered, and that this exemplary passion ought not to be known by me alone.

THURSDAY, AUGUST 1

I've just returned from your burial. The weather was beautiful.

Beautiful in the way you love, with a light breeze that makes the poplars sing. I love you.

Your mother was unbearable, sobbing, shrieking, casting herself down upon your grave. I was smiling; I knew you were resting under the freshly dug earth, that I had to be patient, but that soon you'd be coming back. . . . But don't wait too long, nights without you are unendurable! Don't worry, as I promised you, I'll be good and merry . . . not too good, you know that.

SATURDAY, AUGUST 3

The weather is still lovely. The scent of the white rose bushes fills the courtyard. In the heart of one of the roses, I found a splendid greenish golden-brown beetle. It's been a long time since I've seen one as beautiful as that.

Sunday, August 4

This morning I went out at dawn, crossing the lawn to the terrace. My feet and the hem of my nightgown were wet with dew. Gossamer nets woven by the mist stretched between the rows of pine trees whose planting you had ordered and supervised. A train went chugging by in the distance . . .

A great softness enveloped the hillocks. I was filled with peace and well-being in spite of your absence.

I walked back toward the house, hugging my shawl close to my body. Under my nightgown, the morning coolness hardened my nipples; they ached as they do after your love bites.

Back in the kitchen I heated a little milk. The cat came rubbing himself against my legs, meowing. I shoved him aside with a light kick; I don't want him to touch me. . . . No one but you has the right to touch me, not even the cat. And yet I'm fond of this cat . . .

As always, the milk boiled over. I know how much this annoys you. I do all I can to pay attention, but the milk always boils over.

I poured what was left of it in a bowl with your name on it, the one we purchased at Le Croisic. Do you remember? Pressing my lips against the rim of the heavy crockery, I felt as though I'd caught the shadow of your mouth in mine. The warm liquid was all the more delicious for it.

I took a basket and stepped out into the garden to pick the last of the raspberries. I'll make some jam, adding only enough sugar to let you recall the sour taste and fragrance of this fruit, which you compare to my nipples when you stretch, pinch, wring them so as to make them tender, flushed with the rush of stirred blood.

When I completed my picking, the sun was high and hot. Another day without rain.

In the evening, if the temperature drops, I'll come by to see you.

MONDAY, AUGUST 5

The heat split the earth of your grave and dried out all the flowers. . . . You must have been choking under all that! . . .

I ran to the fountain to get some water. The watering can was so heavy I had to use both hands to carry it. I went back and forth a number of times to wet the thirsty earth. My back and hands were aching.

I sat down on the neighboring gravestone—you remember, that of a poet whose writings left no trace. My black dress was so wet it stuck to my body. I was more than nude since in this heat I wore no underwear. I turned toward you, lifted my dress, opened my thighs wide so you could see my slit and my fleece. I exposed myself as you like me to do. It was so good to feel your eyes on me. . . . The gravestone's roughness bruised my buttocks. I swirled my hips slowly, then faster and faster, without forgetting to open myself until it hurt . . . then I cried out, closing my thighs upon the pleasure you'd given me.

This scared Lulu, the idiot boy who takes care of the cemetery. He ran off holding his huge violet-hued prick in his hand, squealing like a piglet. I was right not to drive him away, wasn't I? You saw he was watching us?

I went back home, tired but happy at the thought of having spent time with you.

I don't know why, but, despite the heat, I woke up with my teeth chattering.

Come back soon. I'm cold without you in our bed.

TUESDAY, AUGUST 6

Today was market day at L. I found ripe, runny Saint-Marcellin cheese at our dairy. The champagne you ordered had not arrived, and I said to M. that you wouldn't like that. He gave me a strange look, sputtering a string of apologies. I purchased *Adolphe* at the bookstore in an inexpensive series. Do you remember telling me to read it? You called it an admirable book. I trust your judgment completely; you've always given me excellent advice as to my reading. . . . At the bookstore I ran into Doctor J., who whispered, with a look full of pity: "Little lady, don't hesitate to call me if you need anything at all. It's good for you to come down to town; you've got to relax, find some recreation."

"This is exactly what my husband keeps telling me: 'Have a bit of fun.'"

You should have seen his expression, as though he had caught sight of a ghost.

"You don't feel good, doctor?" I asked.

"Oh, no. I'm fine . . . just fine."

He ran out of the bookstore, forgetting his newspaper.

"Doctor, doctor!" shouted the saleslady.

But he was walking fast, almost running. . . . Strange man! Fortunately, he's a very good doctor, "devoted," as your mother says.

WEDNESDAY, AUGUST 7

This afternoon your mother and father came to visit. I told them you were out, all smiles, trying to be pleasant, so as to please you. I deserve a good deal of credit, for your mother never stopped repeating through her tears: "But he's dead! . . . He's dead!"

Who is she talking about?

After they left, I went upstairs to make myself lovely for you. I put on my black lace garter belt and the provocative panties you brought me from Paris. I straightened the seam of my stockings in the mirror.

I feel I have lost weight. My thighs seem longer, my belly nicely flat. Only my breasts seem heavier, fuller. It's normal since they are straining toward your lips. Ah, if you only knew! . . .

Fool that I am! You know everything about me. . . . Aren't you the one who made me discover every parcel of my body, teaching me how to derive pleasure from it? My breasts? You molded them, stretching out the nipples to cause delightfully unbearable pain. You imbibed the droplets of blood surging after your pin pricks. I like to bear the marks you imprint on my flesh. And I'm happy to wear the narrow corselets, which you tighten till I can no longer draw breath.

"I want to be able to grasp you between my two hands, to bend you to the breaking point. The more slender your waist, the more apparent the curve of your hips, the splendid roundness of your ass."

Ah! my ass, you do not simply love it, you worship it. I like nothing better than when you make me kneel in front of the fireplace blazing with sweet-smelling vine shoots. Corselet tightly laced, stockings pulled up, hips arched, I offer my ass before you, as you sit comfortably in your armchair, smoking. Sometimes you place something within the dark hole: flowers, feathers, a lit candle. I like having objects sticking up my asshole while you're looking at me . . .

I rotate my pelvis the better to arouse you. You let out a moan. . . . I know that you're unbuttoning your corduroy trousers. I'm all juicy. I back slowly toward you—the game consists in presenting you with only my ass. If I have feathers in it, I rock back and forth to have them tickle the tip of your cock. If it's a lit candle, I manage to scatter some drops of warm wax upon your tightly erect prick. You utter small cries when the hot wax reaches your erect flesh. I moan like a newborn babe calling for its mother's breast. You then tear out what I have in my ass, and rudely take its place. I cry out. . . . You pay my cries no mind, plunging deeper and deeper into me, moving faster and faster. . . . It's so good! We come at the same time, growling like beasts.

Time passes. . . . These are the sweetest moments. You remain within me. . . . I still desire you. Gradually I tighten my muscles round your prick. Soon I feel it harden again. Deeply stirred, you move. No, not there, in front! . . . You turn me over, free my breasts, seize my nipples between your teeth. You bite, twist, stretch, and pinch them . . .

"Bitch, you're too wet. I can't feel you anymore. . . . You'll see how I fill you up . . ."

What are you going to do to me? I'm frightened. . . . I flow with fear!

"So, you want more! Just you wait, you'll get yours, all right! All you can take!"

Three fingers, four, hand, fist. . . . Your hands are large and strong, your fist is the size of the head of a newborn baby. A circular motion forces your way in. Your knuckles dilate and scratch the lining of my belly.

"Look how it goes in. . . . That's what you wanted, you bitch. . . . My cock isn't enough for you. You need my fist, my whole arm!"

I feel drawn and quartered. . . . I look: your forearm has disappeared within me. . . . I try to open myself wider still. . . . Holding me down with your other hand, you straighten yourself up. You get up, carrying me impaled upon your arm. . . . You spread me apart even more. Blood and spunk are running down your arm. You lick this rich mix. . . . Your stiff prick comes hitting against my legs ... I take it between my feet and masturbate it.... I'd like to drink you. Without letting me go, you spread me on the ground and enter my mouth. ... Very quickly you flow between my lips. My cunt closes tight upon your arm. ... I drink you. It's good. I feel as though you're tearing off one of my nipples. ... I let out a shriek! ... IT HURTS! MORE! ... MORE!

After our mad bouts, as you call them, I find myself in our bed, or in a warm bath. You tuck me in, wash me, cajole me till I fall asleep, happy and sated. I love you!

At the cemetery, children playing between the tombs prevented me from staying longer with you. Brats, they interfered with my pleasure!

FRIDAY, AUGUST 9

Stormy weather. Everyone here is watching it fearfully. Right now it seems to be moving elsewhere, where it will explode. One can hear dull thundering far off. Protected from the heat by closed shutters, I'm awaiting the evening to go and join you. I haven't touched the dinner Adrienne left on a tray before my door. I'm hungry only for you.

Nine o'clock rings from the bell tower. It's time to leave for our rendezvous. The heat is still overwhelming. It envelops me completely, climbs up my legs. Soon I'm sweating. The slope leading to the cemetery seems steeper than usual; yet I climb it running in my haste to be near you.

The flowers on your grave are wilted, even burned. I pull them up and cast them on the garbage heap. I run across Lulu, who throws me a sly look. The stridulous song of the crickets and cicadas loses its intensity. The light is fading. White lightning tears through the somber sky, making me jump. Almost at once, it is followed by thunder shaking the ground. I feel its vibrations under my feet. "It hasn't struck too far away, I believe. . . ." A few drops of hot rain fall upon my face. I drink them avidly. Nothing. The sky has suddenly grown light, the storm is receding. . . . No, here's another flash of lightning—this time blue—streaking the sky, followed by another, bright yellow, dazzling, another . . . still another . . . yet another. I burst out laughing: it's going to rain! . . . Indeed, it does, falling on me, on you, on Lulu, who is running over there. I laugh, I dance. . . . Oh, the rain! good rain, warm rain! In an instant, the paths of the cemetery are changed to hundreds of small, raging, torrential streams, running around the trees, flowing over the graves. Feeling it wash over your body, you laugh, as I do, and you dance like me! The earth that covers you is now thick and shiny. I take some in my hands, smearing it on my face. . . . We laugh! . . . The sky has turned black, night has fallen over the countryside. This is a feast night with fireworks and flashes. "Oh, the beautiful blue one! Oh, the lovely yellow one! Oh, the green!" It's far more beautiful than Bastille Day. I tear off my dress and panties, full of desire for you. I straddle your face, rub my vulva against the wet earth. It's so good! I pick up handfuls of earth and stick them up my yawning belly. . . . Pebbles scratch me. I sink. . . . You sink. . . . Yes, still further. Ah, you're making me come! . . . Breathless, I fall upon you. The rain patters on my ass. I lift it up, taking full advantage of it. Two hands seize my hips. Are you the one growling like this? Someone tries to introduce a stick into my anus. My love, it's much too large. You won't be able to do it. Wait, I'm going to help you. Are my buttocks spread far enough? It's better now. You're tearing me apart. Stop, you're crazy! The stick is huge. Ah! . . .

I faint, feeling as though a red-hot iron were singeing my womb. My love, you're a brutal creature indeed. Near us, Lulu is masturbating. I've never seen a phallus like his, immense and knotted. I laugh, thinking of the expression "well hung like a bull." Lulu is indeed like a bull. Seeing me laugh, he laughs with me. His laugh is sharp and sour; it doesn't go at all with his immense member. I continue laughing as he masturbates faster and faster. A first spurt of sperm, then a second bespatter my face. His semen has a strong smell, a bitter taste. I cover my face and breasts with it. Does it excite you, dearest? D'you want him to fuck me? . . .

You always said to me: "One day, I'll have Lulu fuck you." D'you remember?

I always protested: "But he's the village idiot, a fool. I don't want to make love with that!"

"Who's asking you to make love?" you would reply. "It's nothing but a fuck, that's all!"

That's all?! Men don't understand anything about these matters. For us fucking and making love is one and the same. At least for me . . .

"I take pleasure in fucking only if I'm in love."

"What a child you are!" you'd answer.

Today I understand what you wanted to say: one can fuck and climax without loving, or almost. . . . If I'm fucking this monster, it is to please you, and I'll have an orgasm because you'll be looking at me. See how I excite him, how good I am at returning his prick to its impressive volume. What a morsel of flesh! . . .

I hasten to remove the earth from my cunt. I'm covered with mud. Your eyes, his prick! Ah!

The storm is receding, the rain falls gentle and warm. I make an effort to sit up. Everything turns around me. . . . A warm liquid flows out of me, along my thighs. I touch it, lift my fingers to my lips and taste it. It is a mixture of sperm, earth, and blood. . . . I rise with a moan. My torn stockings are hanging round my ankles, my garter belt has vanished. Bent in two, I drag myself to the fountain. I squat under the cool water, which soothes the burning sensation in all my openings. I return to you. My dress is nothing but a dirty, dripping rag. It takes all my strength to slip into it.

"Are you pleased with me, my love? It was wonderful coming like that, wasn't it? I'll come back tomorrow. I hope there'll be another storm. I do love storms."

Sunday, August 18

Forgive me, my love. I wasn't able to keep our appointment. After our glorious night together I was very ill; they thought I would die. Can you imagine, to die at my age? But I overcame this crisis; you would have been so unhappy. We love each other so deeply that if one of us were to die, the other could not survive. Oh, were you to die, my love! . . . This frightful thought causes my fever to rise. Don't worry, I'm not going to die. I won't leave you alone under the earth. . . . Unless, perhaps, I can join you? That's a good idea, isn't it? . . . What do you think?

As soon as I am well, I'll visit you. It's a promise.

Wednesday, August 21

I'm feverish again. It seems I have nightmares every night, calling you, begging you to come for me. The strange thing is that I remember nothing, I, who used to recall every detail of my dreams, both good and bad.

Apparently, I also call for Lulu. Poor Lulu. Since my illness he's been walking in circles around the house, despite Adrienne, who chases him off as soon as she catches sight of him.

SATURDAY, AUGUST 24

I feel better now. The doctor has allowed me to get out of bed.

Lulu has thrown a large bouquet of blue hydrangeas through my bedroom window. I believe they come from the bushes planted round the town hall. It made me laugh. If that's the case, the local paper will write it up.

SUNDAY, AUGUST 25

Caught sight of Lulu hiding in the privet hedge, holding his huge prick. I was alone, stretched out on my chaise longue. I let the light blanket slip and raised my nightgown. He grunted with satisfaction, spreading the leafy boughs to show me his erection. I responded by opening my thighs and caressing myself. At first it was pleasant, but quite soon I was bored. I wanted you to be there, guiding my fingers, telling the idiot boy to fuck me. I pulled the blanket up and started to cry as I hadn't for a long time. The time is too long. I miss you and want to join you where you are. There was a commotion in the privet hedge. Lulu ran off, pursued by Adrienne, shouting: "Swine! Bastard! It's a crying shame! Just you wait and see, I'm going to call the cops!"

Fortunately, Lulu is a fast runner. Adrienne came back to me, short of breath. She misinterpreted my tears.

"Poor child! Look what state you're in, all because of this bastard!"

TUESDAY, AUGUST 27

Your friend Jean called on me; it was nice. Of course we spoke of you, and of the next grape harvest. He is preparing a show for October, and I promised him we'd be there. He gave me a strange look, concerned and moved at the same time. He touched my hair with a halting hand. I was about to recoil, but his caressing touch was pleasant, and his sad and tender expression made me feel like snuggling in his arms.

You're not jealous, are you?

He suggested an outing to the coast when I recover, and I accepted joyfully.

After he left, I stretched out upon our bed. I wanted you so much I started to tremble. I tried to get up in order to go to our meeting place, but I fell back, drained. I haven't recovered yet.

I love you.

WEDNESDAY, AUGUST 28

Doctor J. paid me another visit. He prescribed a tonic and sleeping pills, assuring me that with time I'll feel better.

SUNDAY, SEPTEMBER 1

Your parents took me to the cemetery. You were buried a month ago. You must begin to feel the weight of time down there. Be patient a little longer. I'll soon be near you.

Your mother was snuffling, her face disfigured by her tears. "When a woman weeps," you used to say, "she must manage to be even prettier."

No one told your mother that.

I stretched out upon you, with my lips pressed to the earth to whisper tender words. Your mother's cries kept me from speaking to you, caressing you. Your father lifted me, hugging me to his breast. I felt a tear running down my cheek. He took me in his arms, carried me to the car. I felt good.

TUESDAY, SEPTEMBER 3

I washed my hair, cleared the skin of my face and body of dead cells, and bathed for a long time in bath oil–scented water. I took care of myself, something I have failed to do for a long time now. There is nothing better for the morale than feeling lovely and clean.

Doctor J. came by and was very pleased with me.

You won't hold it against me if I don't go to the cemetery today? I'm overtaken by an immense kind of indolence. I'll lie down in the sun to get a light tan.

THURSDAY, SEPTEMBER 5

It's been a long time since I had such a pleasant day. Jean arrived at nine in the morning, smiling, tanned, wearing white linen trousers and a matching sweater. I was also all in white—you know, my wide skirt buttoned all the way down in the front and a shirt tied at the waist. I had taken a wool jacket because the weather is so unpredictable in September. Adrienne packed us a picnic lunch.

During the drive we hardly spoke. The road ran straight between rows of pine trees. Jean then took a forest dirt road, parking his car near a cabin used as a shelter in the hunting season. He gave me a hand to climb up the dune. His hands are narrow and strong, almost as beautiful as yours. All of a sudden we saw the ocean.

Every time I come upon the sea I experience a kind of shock: I feel my chest expanding as an irresistible urge impels me to run toward it. And that's exactly what I did, shouting joyfully, tumbling down the incline of the dune at full speed, arms flung wide open. I unbuttoned my skirt and took off my blouse on the run.

Since I had my bathing suit on, instead of underwear, I threw myself into the water at once. How cold it was!

Jean joined me, and we swam out to the buoy. Out of breath, we held on to it. I was laughing.

"You're so young and beautiful," Jean said, looking dazzled.

I kept on thinking: He's also young and handsome.

I moved close to him, slipping my legs between his. I put my hand into his trunks, but when I tried to pull off his bathing trunks, he forced me to surface.

"Why?" I asked.

He had a sad little smile.

"He was my friend. I don't want to cheat on him."

What does it have to do with cheating? Men are stupid; they don't understand anything. Fortunately, you're not like that. You like it when I make love with your friends.

Annoyed, I swam toward the deserted shore, fell on the wet sand. The waves lifted me gently. The front of my body was cold, while the sun warmed my back.

Jean lay down next to me. I felt his eyes upon my loins and arched my back. A wave, stronger than the others, projected us against one another. You would have said: "It's a sign." Our legs and arms were entangled. We rolled in the waves. He freed my breasts, rubbing his face against them and sucking on my stiff nipples.

"Bite me," I ordered.

He obeyed, timidly at first.

"Harder!" I shouted.

His teeth sank into my flesh while his fingers squeezed the other breast. I came violently, while he whispered my name through his tears: "Marie . . ."

SATURDAY, SEPTEMBER 7

Last night, pebbles thrown against the shutters of my bedroom woke me up. I looked out and saw Lulu standing with the center of the courtyard. In one hand he held his prick, and with the other his enormous, terrifying dog. Remember you used to say: "If you're not a good girl, I'll have you laid by Lulu's dog. . . ."

I slip into a dress and espadrilles. I go by the door of the room where Adrienne has been sleeping since I got ill. She's snoring, so I can go on my way.

Outside Lulu takes me by the hand. He's striding, so I have a hard time keeping up with his pace. His prick, which he did not bother to put back into his trousers, goes knocking against his thighs. Where is he taking me? It doesn't matter. I'm glad you sent him in search of me. I go where you tell me to go. I've forgotten the dog.

Lulu's house is down the road, at the entrance to the village. He lives with his two brothers, his father, and his crippled mother in a kind of cavern, which used to be a stable. We walk through a courtyard cluttered with all manner of detritus. He pushes a door open, and we enter a dark room. There seems to be no electricity since an oil lamp hangs from the ceiling. Despite the darkness I can make out three men and a woman seated at a long table. I feel their eyes upon me. The men rise and draw closer. A sudden blaze of light allows them to emerge from the shadows; someone must have thrown an armful of vine shoots into the fireplace. I examine these men with curiosity. They're as tall as Lulu, but they possess a mean expression he doesn't have. I smile at them. The oldest man, undoubtedly the father, proffers a sticky glass of red wine, ordering:

"Drink, it's good stuff."

I empty the glass in one gulp. It's true that the wine is good. The man fills my glass again. I don't turn it down; I'm thirsty.

However, I now drink it slowly, savoring it knowledgeably. I don't dare refuse the third glass. After the fourth I feel so hot I'd like to take off my dress. The mother, a disgusting witch, drinks greedily. Wine flows down her chin; she belches and farts.

"Behave yourself, old woman," says her husband. "There's a lady here!"

She farts harder than ever. Everyone bursts out laughing.

I'm hot. Sweat is running down between my breasts, along my armpits. Lulu picks up the bottom of my dress to raise it. I wriggle to help him take it off. Now I'm naked, and I drink.

One of the brothers produces a harmonica. I begin to dance. Lulu also, if you call it dancing, his bearlike rocking in place. With every movement, his erection hits his belly. The father pulls my head back, forcing me to drink. I laugh, splattered with wine. The two brothers lay me down upon the table. One of them holds my arms, while the other spreads my legs apart. Why are they doing this? Don't I look receptive? You wouldn't approve, my love, were I to reject these dirty, stinking men, you who always wished to take me into the woods, or on the side of a road, to have me fucked by strangers. I never accepted, but today I'm intent on pleasing you. I'm going to climax through every aperture in my body!

The first to screw me is the father, whose member is in no way inferior to Lulu's. He quickly dispatches his business, which won't do for me. One of the sons is next. Ah, that's better! The other brother and Lulu don't miss a thing. I carry Lulu's cock to my lips, covering it with small licks. It's out of the question to stick it in my mouth; it's huge. I stroke the other brother's balls. The one who's fucking me ejaculates, uttering sharp little cries. The one I was masturbating turns me over on my stomach and raises my ass. He slips his fingers into my cunt and covers his prick with my spunk. Spreading my buttocks, he slips into my anus. Lulu slips under me and tries to stick his tool into my belly. I'm so wet and so full from behind that he must do it again and again. At last he succeeds. Invigorated by this spectacle, the other brother sticks his gluey member into my mouth. All my holes are full up.

I love! You love? . . .

They explode at the same time. My whole body is coming. The room fills with the smell of piss, sperm, shit, and washy wine. In her corner, the crippled hag, skirts raised, utters small rabbit squeals. I'm floating . . .

The dog is barking wildly, standing up on his back paws to get up on the table. The father helps him: "Look at the bastard. He wants his share!"

The four men burst out laughing, slapping their thighs, which sets their loose-hanging pricks in motion. The men turn me over, and have me kneel on all fours. I feel the dog's cold snout sniffing me. It gives me long licks. I turn to look at the animal and see a long red member coming out of its hirsute body. Its paws with their sharp claws are resting on my shoulders, while hands help the creature enter me. The dog's member reaches into the depths of my belly; I feel it growing larger within me. It bites the nape of my neck with such violence that I faint . . .

When I recover my senses, I see the dog resting in front of the fireplace, licking the tip of its cock. The men are laughing and drinking, their pricks hanging loose out of their trousers. The father walks over to me to pour wine between my legs before letting it run straight down my throat. This gives him an idea: he pushes the bottle into my vagina. It's cold. He's pushing so hard I fear it'll break. His three sons egg him on: "C'mon, Dad, the bitch just eats it up."

But he's too drunk. He lets the bottle drop to the ground and break. Then all of them throw themselves on me. I no longer know who's fucking me: bottles, pricks, the dog, the hag . . .

I feel as though I'd been bludgeoned. I open my eyes. A weak ray of light is filtering in under the door. It must be morning. I've got to get home or Adrienne will be furious. I'm lying on the ground. I'm cold. An awful pain in my belly and my ass force me to fall back again. I try breathing deeply, calmly. The pain is receding. I get up on my feet by hanging on to the table. The bottom of my body is encrusted with dry blood. Everything around me is whirling. The few steps I take require an effort you can't imagine. The pain is back, but it is now bearable. Naked, covered with dust, vomit, and excrement, I look for my dress, unable to find it. There's a long cape hanging on a hook near the door, the kind shepherds used to wear. I take it off the hook, covering myself with it. It's stiff with dirt and smells of mud. I cast a last look at the hovel wherein you led me. The four half-naked men are lying in a heap in a corner of this lair. The old woman is still where she was. She moves her arms in my direction. No sound comes from her toothless, rotting mouth. The dog looks up and wags its tail. I open the door.

The cool freshness of dawn reawakens some of my strength. The air smells of mint and citronella. The sky is rosy. A little blood runs down my legs. I feel good. I am hardly aware of the stones of the path I follow. My bare feet carry me, weightless. Skeins of mist hang on the vines. A light wind strums the poplar trees, making them hum, and blows in my direction the odor of burnt wood. I am full of an immense well-being.

The house is still asleep. I'm able to reach the bathroom without awakening Adrienne. After locking the door, I open wide the bathtub faucets. The heavy cape falls at my feet. Who is this creature I catch sight of in the mirror, smiling, wildly disheveled? She seems to have emerged from a suspense film. I burst out laughing, realizing this creature is me! Be happy, your buddies have done some job on me!

I sprinkle geranium and rose bath salts into the tub's rushing water. Next, I wash my hair under the shower, and, having rinsed it, I proceed to rub a conditioner into my scalp to make my hair shiny and soft again.

All of a sudden I feel very weary. I immerse myself in the water, holding on to the sides of the tub. I feel as though I were melting in the hot liquid. No! It would be too stupid to faint at this moment. I bite my lips. The blue water has turned red. I remain a few minutes without moving, then I clean myself thoroughly, careful not to overlook any part of my aching, sated body.

I step out of the tub, draping your beige bathrobe around me. I empty the tub of its repulsively murky water. I decide not to use the dryer on my hair so as not to wake Adrienne. Without removing your bathrobe I slip into our bed.

I fall asleep at once.

MONDAY, SEPTEMBER 9

I slept for fifteen uninterrupted hours. I feel at the top of my form. Adrienne couldn't believe her eyes, seeing me devour the buttered toast and ask for more. You're absolutely right when you say that there's nothing like a screw to stimulate the appetite. You recall how annoyed I used to be when you said things like that at the start of our marriage. I thought you were vulgar. What a silly I was!

TUESDAY, SEPTEMBER 10

I saw clearly that your mother was shocked when I came into the living room wearing the low-cut, red cotton dress you bought for me in Ibiza. I even think I heard her grumble in that shrill tone that never fails to exasperate me: "This is not the right look for a young widow!"

Who does she mean? Why is she all in black when she hates that color? Who's a widow?...The stormy weather is driving her up the wall.

However, it's quite understandable. The least bit of motion becomes unbearably painful in this heat. It's like mid-July. But in the living room, with its shutters closed, the temperature is pleasant. Adrienne brings in ice-cold beverages. We drink in silence.

At last your mother left, giving me a faint kiss. But your dad held me tight against his chest.

WEDNESDAY, SEPTEMBER 11

I dismissed Adrienne, and she accepted gratefully.

"I'll be able to sleep at last. I haven't slept a wink since your illness."

I almost burst out laughing in her face remembering hearing her snores all the way in my room, night after night. Seized with scruples, she inquired:

"Are you sure you're able to remain alone, that you won't need anything?"

"Didn't Doctor J. say I was out of the woods?"

For her, what the good doctor says is gospel truth. Her mind at rest, she left.

At last I'll be able to think only of us, to be all yours. This evening I'll join you.

THIS EVENING, ELEVEN O'CLOCK AT NIGHT

I washed up carefully, perfuming my whole body. My hair, brushed for a long time, is shining. I've put on the white cinch belt I wore on our wedding day, and matching silk stockings. I tied the ribbons of my gold, high-heeled slippers round my ankles. I'm ready. I've swallowed all the pills prescribed by Doctor J. In a matter of moments I'll be with you.

◎

The following lines are hardly legible
    The storm is raging . . . lightning illumines the path leading to the cemetery . . . the wind shakes and bends the trees of the garden . . . lightning follows lightning . . . one can see as clearly as in broad daylight. . . . I feel tired . . . my head is spinning . . . I'm hot, I'm cold. . . . Split in two by lightning, the old elm cracks and falls . . . all of nature has become a gigantic St. Vitus dance . . . the wind sweeps into my room, lifts my hair . . . I hear your voice calling me . . . it's hard for me to keep my eyes open . . . you open your arms. . . . My legs are numb . . . I'm coming, my love . . . I'm coming . . . an icy bliss fills my being . . . I love you . . . I love you . . .

◎

While posted on the border between Tonkin and China, I heard of the death, a few weeks apart, of my young aunt and her husband. She was my mother's young sister; we were just three years apart. Since the death of my parents, she was my only family. I returned to France eighteen months after her demise. Being her sole heir, I went to see our family notary at B. After expressing his deepest sympathy, he handed me the keys of the estate I had inherited, saying:
    "What a sad event, such a young woman!"
    "How did she die?" I inquired.
    "Killed by lightning."
    I took my car and drove to the estate. A quinquagenarian maid greeted me. Warned of my coming by the notary, she had opened the windows. Despite this precaution, a musty odor pervaded the rooms.

"Were you there at the time of the death of my aunt and her hus-band?"

"Yes, the poor gentleman died of cancer six months after his mar-riage, and madame a month later, killed by the storm."

I asked her to leave me alone in the house, and I then inspected it. I opened the drawers of the secretary in the bedroom; one of them was double bottomed. I slipped in my hand and took out a notebook with a black linen cover, a collection of the writings of Thérèse de l'Enfant Jésus, and some thirty typewritten pages, carefully corrected in schoolgirl fash-ion in blue ink. They were signed Pierre Angélique and entitled: The Dead Man. On the title page I read: MARIE REMAINED ALONE WITH THE DEAD EDOUARD. Marie was my aunt's Christian name, Edouard that of her husband.

I went on with my reading:

"When Edouard fell back dead, a void opened within her being, a shudder ran through her, rising like an angel. Her naked breasts were standing up in a dream church wherein she experi-enced the knowledge of something irretrievable. Standing by the side of the dead man, absent, floating above herself in a kind of slow ecstasy, she was filled with dismay. She knew she was des-perate, but she also toyed with that sentiment. Edouard, as he lay dying, had begged her to strip naked.

She had not been able to carry out this wish in time! There she was, disheveled, with only her breasts spilling out of her torn dress.

∽

I felt uneasy, yet I pursued my reading. When I was through, I stayed there for a while, my heart beating fast. I was surrounded by these pages strewn upon the bed. My mouth filled with a taste of ashes as I read the final words of this strange text, which kept on knocking within my head: "Only the sun remained."

I got up and walked to the window. I could see vineyards, fields, and forests spreading before me, bathed by the soft glow of the soothing autumn light. The landscape reflected the hand of man and the obstinate toil of generations. I went back to the secretary and took out the poems of Thérèse Martin. The thin volume fell open to a page where a passage had been framed in red pencil:

> Beloved, do not deprive me of your gentle smile
> I need to hide within your heart awhile
> Assuaging thus my boundless desire
> Of consummation by the sweetest fire.
> Oh blissful moment! Joy ineffable!
> When I shall hear a voice so affable
> And glimpse at last the Face I can adore
> Radiant with light divine forever more.

I remained perplexed. What did Marie Françoise Thérèse Martin, the French Carmelite nun known as the Little Flower of Lisieux, have to do with Pierre Angélique?

I opened the black notebook and saw on the first page, written in printed letters: "THE STORM." I sat down and read.

After my reading I remained deep in thought. What should I do with this notebook: destroy it, keep it, publish it? I left the room, carrying like a thief the contents of the secret drawer.

I left for B. without having made up my mind one way or the other.

According to the notebook, she was not killed by lightning: she committed suicide. Why do they all say the opposite?

The following day I went to the offices of the local paper and asked to consult the issues of September 12 and the following days. This is what I found:

Killed by Lightning One Month After Her Husband's Death

The lifeless body of the young Madame D., twenty-six years old, was discovered in the vineyard surrounding the family estate on the night between September 11 and 12. The nude body did not bear any trace of wounds or violence. After examining the body, the medical expert concluded that the young woman had beem struck by lightning, which explains why she was found naked, since her clothing must have been destroyed by the thunderbolt that caused her death. Madame D. had lost her spouse, dead of a dreadful disease, a short time after their marriage. The editors wish to express their sympathy and share the family's mourning.

Leafing aimlessly through the papers I found the following notice:

In the Woods of M. Children Discover a Man Who Hanged Himself

Eric and Michel, eight and ten years old, who were playing hide-and-seek in the M. woods, found the body of Lucien R., otherwise known as Lulu, hanging from the branch of an oak tree. The simple-minded young man had been given by the commune the public office of tending the cemetery of M. There is no doubt as to the cause of death: suicide. However, a ghastly detail amazed the police: the unfortunate man wore round his neck a white lace garter belt. He must have stolen it from a neighbor's laundry line.

Translator's note: Pierre Angélique was the pseudonym used by the writer Georges Bataille, author of numerous erotic writings, as well as famous essays on eroticism. Between 1941 and 1945 he used this name to publish Madame Edwarda, *which finally was brought out by Jean-Jacques Pauvert in 1956, still under this pseudonym. Bataille signed only the preface with his real name. Pauvert and Deforges are close friends and have been associates in numerous censorship trials. Indeed, this novella bears the stamp of both Pauvert and Bataille.*

Made in
Hong Kong

"*C*ards."

Jeanne's hoarse voice seemed more muffled than usual. The manager of the club had been standing behind her for a long while, watching her lose. What would her husband, the minister, say when his wife's debts were called in? This thought brought a nasty smile to the thin lips of Mr. George, as he was known to his employees. A tall man, almost thin, he had a cultivated elegance, but a subtly excessive fastidiousness betrayed a certain coarseness of mind. He would have been attractive, had he not the thick hands of a killer, and that hard gaze, which softened only when he reveled in his malice.

Presently his eyes were traveling from her slender, carefully manicured hands, whose every motion set off flashes from a superb sapphire ring and the diamonds of her wedding band, to her bare shoulders rising from her crimson taffeta evening gown.

Wearily letting the cards drop from her lovely hands, she cast a bewildered look about her. She must have been insane. In the space of a few hours, she had lost more than twenty thousand francs! The day before she'd lost the same amount, and the day before that. . . . How much did she owe George? She refused to permit herself to add it up. How could she possibly repay such a sum? She couldn't discuss it with Jacques. He was fed up with settling her gambling debts and had threatened to divorce her if it ever happened again. She knew that this time it was for real. Although his ministerial appointment was recent, he'd stick to his word. Better to risk becoming a mere deputy than to further deplete a fortune that was already nothing but a myth. By the tone of George's voice when he loaned her the sum she had just lost, she knew she could no longer count on him. Turn to her friends? Out of the question—she already owed them too much money! This time it was over—she'd never gamble again!

She took her beaded bag, her lighter and cigarettes, and rose wearily. Her whole body felt heavy, bruised. She bumped into George, who stepped aside to let her pass.

"I'd like to speak with you. Would you please follow me into my office?"

Jeanne agreed and followed him through the gaming rooms.

"Place your bets, gentlemen, place your bets . . ."

"All bets are down."

"Six wins."

Jeanne thought: I should have played roulette. George took a key out of his pocket and opened a padded, green leather door.

"Come in, please sit down. What will you have to drink? Scotch, champagne, port?"

"A little champagne, please."

"Do you like pink champagne? I've an excellent one."

He took a bottle from a refrigerator, hidden behind a facade of fake book bindings, and reached for a tray and two glasses, which he placed on a corner of his desk. The pop of the cork startled Jeanne from her dark thoughts. As he poured, some of the foam ran down the sides of the glasses. He handed one to Jeanne, who gulped it down. He poured her another. Sipping his slowly, he settled down behind his desk with a bored expression.

Sitting in one of the two armchairs, Jeanne inquired, "Did you wish to speak with me?"

"Yes, I'm actually very embarrassed. You owe me one hundred fifty thousand francs. I need that money."

"But I don't have that much!"

"Ask your husband . . ."

"You know better than anyone that my husband has forbidden me to gamble and that he'll refuse to pay."

"He has no other choice."

Jeanne got up angrily.

"Are you threatening me?"

"Please don't take that tone. I need that money, and you've got to return it to me."

Close to tears, Jeanne sat down again.

"It's impossible, you know that!"

"Sell your jewelry."

"I've already done that. With what money do you think I pay you back every time?"

"What about this ring?"

"It belonged to Jacques's mother. He's attached to it."

"I'm sorry, but I must call your husband."

George consulted his Rolodex, lifted the receiver, and dialed. "Stop!"

The phone was ringing.

"Stop, I beg you. I'll do anything you want."

Slowly, he hung up and looked at Jeanne, very pale, standing with her hands flat on the desk. She was one of the most beautiful women he had ever seen: magnificent tawny blond, almost red hair, very light green eyes, a classic oval face, a dimpled chin, a perfect nose, a mouth that men longed to bite, the long-legged body of a thoroughbred with high, full breasts. Moreover, she had a refinement, an intelligence, a sense of humor that made her one of the most sought-after women in Paris. A member of one of the oldest Protestant families from Vendée, she had inherited from her father the same taste for gambling that had poisoned her childhood, ruined her mother, and culminated in her father's suicide. She gambled as if drugged, throwing caution to the winds. She had been barred from playing for years, but her passion drove her to dives or café back rooms. Once, having inadvertently provoked a fight, she was stabbed and seriously wounded. This cured her of poker games with bistro thugs, but not of gambling. As soon as she left the hospital, the bar to her gambling having expired, she returned to the green tables of the casinos and the clubs. In spite of her love for her husband and her promise never to touch a card again, she could not shake her "costly vice," as her mother used to say. George knew the whole story. She had once scornfully rejected him, when he had hinted that there were many ways of settling her debts. Since then, he had sworn to get even.

"I have an assignment for you. If you accept, I'll give you back all the chits you've signed."

"What's involved? Am I to run drugs for you?"

Jeanne's tone was so scornful that George had a hard time restraining himself.

"You've got a low opinion of me. It has nothing to do with drugs. But, let's drop the subject . . ."

He reached for the telephone.

"Forgive me, I'm tired, I don't know what I'm saying. What's it about?"

"It involves carrying documents—nothing secret, but I want to be sure that they're placed in the proper hands, signed in front of you, and brought back by you."

"Where do I have to go?"

"To Hong Kong."

"To Hong Kong? But that's the end of the world . . ."

"You'll tell your husband that Madam Wong, your antique dealer friend, can't travel to Hong Kong for health reasons, and that she's asked you to go in her place."

"You've thought it all out!"

"All of it. Do you know Hong Kong? No? Neither do I. They say it's a fantastic place."

"When must I leave?"

"Oh . . . sometime next week. Let's say Tuesday. OK? I'll have your ticket sent to you. This time of year the weather's very mild in Hong Kong."

. . . During one of your trips to Paris, you expressed the desire that your contracts be brought by a very attractive young woman. I've entrusted these papers to one of my friends. She's ravishing, blond, and very elegant. Her only fault is her uncontrollable love of gambling. I hope she'll appeal to you; she's entirely at your disposal. She will arrive on . . .

Lotus, a very young and beautiful Chinese girl, was seated entirely naked on a pile of cushions. She had just finished reading the letter aloud and now placed it in her lap, awaiting a response. It would be difficult to imagine a more monstrous figure than the Chinese man who was her audience. His enormous mass spilled over a low divan, while two very pretty, bare-breasted, young Thai women massaged him. Truong, for that was his name, must have weighed close to 450 pounds. The expert touch of his masseuses' fingers elicited small grunts of satisfaction from him. A burst of laughter from him startled the Chinese girl.

"George will do anything to close a deal. If this woman is as beautiful as he says, I'll really enjoy myself. What do you think, Lotus?"

"I thought, master, that you didn't like white women . . ."

"Yes, but this one seems special. Even Tchou, who saw her at George's, raved about her. . . . She might even be able to revive in me some of the vigor you're no longer able to arouse, bitch!"

He threw at her a superb vase that had been resting on a low table near him. It broke at Lotus's feet without touching her. He shook off the masseuses with a shrug of his shoulders. Gathering a sumptuous silk robe, the girls wrapped him in it. Lotus nestled into him, rubbing against him like a young animal. Next to this mountain of flesh she seemed tiny.

"Master, I've got a surprise for you. . . . Tonight I'm going to bring you a piece that's missing from your collection."

Truong's face lit up.

"That's good news." Then, angrily, he pushed her away upon the cushions. "Idiot, if you tell me about it, it's no longer a surprise!"

He left the room, wrapping the embroidered silk robe around the bulging folds of his body. One of the masseuses draped a golden kimono over Lotus's shoulders.

∞

Lotus took the star ferry for Kowloon, then the double-decker bus to Salisbury Road, and got off at Jordan Road. She wore the black cotton trousers and tunic of the poor elderly women of Aberdeen and Repulse Bay. But on her, the simple and functional clothing had the look of having come from one of the elegant Mandarin or Peninsula tailor shops. She headed for Nanking Street and turned down Reclamation Street. It was a very lively small street with open-air restaurants, fruit stands, a large tinware store and notions shop, the street tailor, a Chinese herbal pharmacy, and an antique shop, its window crowded with golden Buddhas, porcelain gods, inlaid pearl screens, jade bracelets, mandarin robes, and fans. Lotus stepped through a narrow door and found herself between two walls lined with disparate objects. Their brilliant gold shone in the shadows. From behind one of the walls a very elderly man, wearing an old-fashioned, long gray robe, suddenly appeared. He bowed several times. His emaciated hands traced complex arabesques in the air as he spoke very rapidly, nodding his head. When he smiled, he revealed toothless jaws. He took out a long, red-lacquer box lined with black silk in which lay a magnificent jade *olisbos,* a penis statuette. Lotus lifted the object from its jewel case and gazed upon it a long while.

"It's really very beautiful."

The old man laughed with delight.

"It's a unique piece, worthy of the greatest museums of the world. It seems that it belonged to one of our empresses. I received it from Peking two days ago. The American ambassador, the French cultural attaché, and even Sir Stephen, the queen's cousin, offered me a fortune for it. But I consider it an honor to be able to sell it to my compatriot Mr. Truong."

Lotus took from her trouser pocket a wad of American dollars. The old man grabbed it, nodding as he counted them. Giggling with satisfaction, he slipped them into one of his wide sleeves.

"That's it, it's all here," said he, wrapping the jewel box and handing it to Lotus.

∞

Jeanne was impressed by the landing on the runway at the Hong Kong airport and was relieved to set foot at last on Chinese soil. Several men turned around to look at her, noting the young woman's charms. A Chinese wearing the uniform of a rich man's chauffeur, accompanied by a customs officer, bowed to her.

"Madame Jacques Descarpes?"

"Yes?"

"I am Mr. Truong's chauffeur—he sent me to fetch you. This is Mr. Cheong, thanks to whom the formalities of customs will be eased."

The customs officer said a few words in Chinese to the chauffeur and indicated that she should follow him. Jeanne retrieved her luggage in record time and soon found herself settled in a superb, newly minted Rolls. She was looking at a city she did not know, the elegant Chinese lettering of its shop signs conferring a festive character to the most ordinary of facades. They turned into the tunnel to cross Causeway Bay. The traffic was heavy and a dense crowd strolled along the sidewalks at the foot of the skyscrapers. Farther on, the traffic grew lighter. They were now traveling uphill along wide avenues lined with handsome apartment buildings and gardens. Soon they found themselves above the bay of Hong Kong. Jeanne fell at once under the spell of so much beauty. The car continued its climb, stopping at last in front of a wide, dark green, wooden gate topped by a tiled roof in the traditional Chinese style. The gate opened, and the car rolled a few moments between hibiscus hedges, coming to a stop in front of a vast residence, its roof covered by glazed green tiles adorned with dragons that seemed to keep watch over the premises.

Dressed in red and black silk pajamas, Lotus, flanked by three pink-pajamaed handmaidens, was awaiting their arrival. The chauffeur opened the car door, and Jeanne stepped out, casting a look around her. Lotus stepped forward with a bow.

"The Honorable Madame Jacques Descarpes?"

Jeanne smiled. "I am the Honorable Madame Jacques Descarpes, but my first name is Jeanne."

"Would Madame Jeanne Descarpes kindly follow me to her bedchamber, where she will be able to rest from her travels. Monsieur Truong, my master, would like to know whether you would honor him by accepting his invitation to dinner tonight?"

∞

A procession of succulent dishes, one smoothly following another, came pouring out of the kitchen. The epicurean Jeanne had almost forgotten the repugnant appearance of her host, whose white dinner jacket only emphasized his monstrous girth.

"You have a remarkable chef."

"A flattering compliment coming from a French lady, and more particularly from one with your refined tastes . . ."

To gather her courage, Jeanne had had quite a bit to drink. Her eyes shone strangely. A very handsome woman, she was wearing a red satin sheath with a high slit in the front, revealing the sumptuous curves of her elegant body. In a tone at once dreamy and provocative, she said, looking straight into Truong's eyes: "Yes, I love all that is precious and rare, objects and moments."

"I share your feelings. I own a very handsome collection of rare objects. Would you care to see it? It is really quite unique. In fact, this very afternoon I received an extremely rare piece."

"With pleasure."

Truong got up from the table and called one of the servants to help Jeanne. She followed the fat Chinaman up to the entrance of a secret room, veiled by a heavy drapery. Behind the curtain an armor-plated door, like that of a bank vault, swung open. Truong stepped back, making way for Jeanne.

The hall she entered was dark. Gradually, she made out in the shadows a magnificent Buddha, radiating the golden light of a sweet wisdom. Its beauty dispelled Jeanne's apprehension. Suddenly, on the right, a spotlight cast its glow from the ambient dark, shining upon an average-height, amethyst *olisbos,* while on the left rose an impressively large phallus of polished ivory, standing upon a pedestal of tangled female bodies. A lacy one, carved in coral, stood near a menacing ebony counterpart. One of silver was bizarrely topped by a globe, while needles sprouted from a gold one. . . . Each spotlight in turn revealed a masterpiece of erotic art. A dazzled Jeanne contemplated in silence these precious reproductions of the male phallus. She was surrounded by *olisboi* carved from various materials, including a modest straw one among these treasures. They were of all sizes. Jeanne walked from one to the other, prey to a strange emotion she tried to control.

"Here's my latest acquisition," Truong said, pointing to a jade *olisbos* resting upon a pedestal placed in front of its jewel case.

"What a beauty! Where do all these marvels come from?"

"Mostly from China. Only a highly civilized, intensely refined people could have produced these magnificent objects. However, some of them come from Africa, Egypt, ancient Rome, India, and Japan. Almost all of them have been used," he added, staring hard into Jeanne's eyes.

"All . . . ," she whispered, absentmindedly stroking a gigantic phallus.

"Almost all, and particularly this one," he said, caressing it lightly with his shapeless hand, whose fingers nevertheless possessed a curiously delicate touch.

They were looking at one another in silence, without ever ceasing to stroke this impressive object. Truong was the first to speak: "These were used to stretch women who were too narrow. Those to punish adulterous wives."

He pointed out a series of average-size, harmless-looking *olisboi*. Lifting one up, he brought out with an imperceptible touch of his hand a cluster of needles and barbs. Jeanne drew back at the sight of the fat Chinaman's cruel smile.

"You must be tired. I'll have you taken to your room. We'll see each other tomorrow. Sleep well. I'll summon Lotus."

He kissed her hand, watching her leave in the company of the young Chinese woman.

Two young servant girls were waiting to help her undress in a room whose luxurious comfort had no trace of the Asiatic about it. Deeply weary, almost lethargic, Jeanne abandoned her body to their care.

"Your beauty fully lives up to the description of it in Monsieur George's letter," Lotus remarked.

Jeanne turned round, smiling: "You're very lovely yourself. Who are you?"

Lotus let the servants know they were no longer needed. She held out to Jeanne a richly embroidered kimono, kneeling before her as she answered: "I'm Mr. Truong's mistress and his slave. He bought me from my parents when I was ten years old. He likes to try out his *olisboi* on me. With one of them he deflowered me a couple of days after purchasing me."

"Do you hate him?"

"No . . . why?"

Jeanne held Lotus's face between her hands, kissing her lightly on the lips.

"Leave me now. I'm sleepy."

Lotus rose seemingly reluctantly from her kneeling posture and walked slowly to the door.

The following morning, Truong and Jeanne had breakfast

on a terrace overlooking the bay. Both wore long, brightly colored mandarin robes. Next to them, spread out upon the table, lay the contracts Jeanne was supposed to have him sign.

"We'll see to this later. First you must visit Hong Kong, the Sung Dynasty Village founded in 960, the Lin Yan monastery on Lantau Island, the new territories, and you must tour the islands on my boat. You'll pay a visit to my friend Chow on Humphrey's Avenue, the greatest dealer in pearls in all of Hong Kong. Next you'll go gambling in Macao—"

Jeanne interrupted him coldly: "I have no wish to gamble."

"As you wish, dear lady. Let's forget about Macao. There are enough clandestine gambling clubs here for your entertainment, if that is your wont. Nothing comparable to Macao, yet deserving of being seen. Lotus is well acquainted with these places, and she'll be happy to show them to you. Alas, my business affairs keep me busy all day; otherwise, I would have deemed it an honor to accompany you. I ordered the car for eleven. Do these arrangements meet with your approval?"

"Perfectly. As to the contracts . . ."

"No hurry! Lotus . . . Lotus! Ah, here you are. Please take Madame Descarpes shopping at Chow's and then to 'the thieves' market.' You'll have lunch at the Mandarin. I've reserved a table for you . . ."

When by the end of the afternoon they returned to Truong's villa, Jeanne was exhausted but delighted with her day. Leaving the car and chauffeur, she and Lotus had covered Kowloon backward and forward. They returned with an armload of purchases. Lotus would not allow Jeanne to pay for anything, saying that Mr. Truong would be very angry and hurt were she to do so. Somewhat annoyed by such excessive hospitality, Jeanne had kept her expenditures within strict limits.

After taking a relaxing bath, she dressed for dinner. As on the previous day, it was lavish. Truong had invited some of his friends. As the evening grew late, Jeanne retired to her room, falling into a deep, dreamless sleep.

The following day, Lotus and Jeanne toured the islands. In the evening, Lotus suggested they visit Hong Kong by night. The car dropped them off at the port of Aberdeen. There, Lotus hailed a frail skiff rowed by a very aged woman who took them to an immense red and gold building, aglow with light. Its restaurant was recommended in the guidebook. They were greeted by the owner, who led them through a maze of corridors, stairways, and dimly lit halls, till they reached a smoke-filled room, buzzing with the voices of some hundred people, mostly Chinese, seated or standing at the gambling tables. Jeanne turned to head back; however, whether in Rome, London, Paris, or Hong Kong, she found the lure of gambling rooms irresistible. Unable to stifle a mounting desire, she lingered.

"You've guessed my weakness."

"Come," said Lotus with an imperceptible smile upon her smooth face, empty of reflection or judgment. Taking out of her pocket an impressive roll of American dollars, she walked up to the cashier's desk in order to change the bills. Jeanne opened her pocketbook.

"I've got money, too."

"Never mind. You're Mr. Truong's guest."

Their hands full of chips, they walked amid the gambling tables.

"What do you want to play? Roulette, baccarat?"

"Last time I lost playing baccarat," Jeanne reflected. "Perhaps ill luck has left me since my departure from Paris . . ."

"Baccarat."

There were two empty spots at the baccarat table. They settled down in them, causing the ripple of a swiftly vanishing curiosity among the players. Lotus was playing with a kind of indifference. As to Jeanne, after an initial stroke of good luck, she kept losing continuously. Soon, the wad of money handed her by Lotus had melted away. Next, she extracted her own money from her pocketbook. The cashier changed it for her, and she went on playing. Having lost once more, she turned abruptly to her companion, who, though standing by her side, had stopped playing. A curt request issued from her very guts: "More money!" Without uttering a word, Lotus handed her a roll of paper money. A sudden tension settled over the gambling table; silence reigned, broken only by the players' orders. All eyes were directed at this beautiful woman in her elegant white silk suit. She was playing with a passion so intense, despite an outer show of self-control, that it surfaced violently, capturing the enthralled attention of those who shared this boundless need. As though the better to mock her, chance allowed her to win once, twice. Then she began to lose again. Her heart was beating fast, her hands were sweating, beads of perspiration covered her brow. Her eyes sought out the young Chinese woman, who seemed to have disappeared. The man who had initially greeted them leaned toward her, handing her a fistful of chips.

"Miss Lotus had to go. She left these for you."

For an instant, Jeanne was ashamed of the sense of relief flooding her being.

"Cards, please!"

Her parched throat ached, as did her eyes, irritated by the smoke of hundreds of cigarettes. Very quickly again she lost. Turning to the man, who was still standing behind her, she caught his negative response. Nothing was forthcoming.

Jeanne felt enveloped by an icy wave. She grew aware of the immense fatigue within her, the result of hours of sustained attention. Gathering every bit of remaining energy, she was able to rise. She must have been deathly pale, since a young Chinese man stepped forward to hold her up.

"A glass of water, please."

"My name is Li Tsé-tung. Miss Lotus has left a message for you. Here, take a sip."

He handed her a glass brought by a waiter. He let her drink before transmitting Lotus's note: "I'm hungry. Ask Li Tsé-tung to accompany you to Mao."

"If you'll be good enough to follow me, I'll take you to where your friend is."

∞

Weary, disgusted with herself, Jeanne huddled on the seat of the tiny junk. She did not have the strength to examine the skiffs loaded with women and children despite the late hour—these floating restaurants, this aquatic city. She let herself be led without the slightest desire to know where she was being taken. People were sleeping on the decks of ships, awakened at times by the sound of a passing motor. The junk now moved through a tangle of canals from which rose the pungent odor of sludge and rotten fish. After a rather long while, it stopped by the side of a much larger junk. Some light filtered through disjointed boards. They moored alongside. Li Tsé-tung helped Jeanne to climb aboard. They entered a room so smoke filled one could not see the back of it. A dim light emphasized the strangeness of the place. Men with strange, frightening faces, seated around a long table inscribed with partially erased Chinese characters, raised their eyes as she entered, staring at the newcomer. Jeanne instinctively backed away. Someone pushed her into the room. All of a sudden Lotus was by her side, her inexpressive visage somehow more childlike among these men whose faces were marked by extreme stupidity, cruelty, baseness. Jeanne could not look at them without a shudder of fear and disgust. Lotus handed her a glass full of some golden liquid.

"Drink, you're very pale. This will do you good."

Unquestioningly, mechanically she obeyed, downing the liquid. A peachy flavor filled her mouth. Lotus was looking at her, smiling.

"I'm certain you'll like this place. It's rather special. What you gamble here is yourself. I suggested to these gentlemen that you might be the stake. If you win, you pocket the money. If you lose, you'll have to grant each and every one what he demands. Do you accept?"

"You must be crazy!"

"Not at all. You'll see. It's very easy."

"And if I refuse?"

"You don't have any choice in the matter. If I were you, I'd accept. They've already paid a lot of money for the privilege of playing with you . . ."

Jeanne glanced all around her, hopelessly seeking assistance. There was no one there she could turn to.

"What will Mr. Truong say when he finds out . . . ?"

"This boat belongs to him."

She showed no anger, as though none of this any longer concerned her. She sat down in the seat pointed out to her by the young Chinese woman, who explained the rules of the game to her in a couple of words. The leader of the table shook three dice in his hand, uttering a long cry, like that of a peacock. The game began. For a whole hour Jeanne was winning.

Then she began to lose. She did not understand at first when a young, one-eyed Chinese man lifted her out of her seat, forcing her back upon the table strewn with chips, loaded with beer glasses, rice brandy, ashtrays spilling their butts. She struggled briefly, but Lotus whispered in her ear: "Watch out, they don't like cheats here!"

Tears were flowing upon Jeanne's cheeks and down her neck. She felt with horror the humid hands of the man pull up her skirt and push aside her panties. She uttered a cry as she felt herself penetrated by his thin, hard penis. She clenched convulsively the edge of the table. To ease the operation, the one-eyed man lifted her legs, keeping them wide open. The onlookers started to laugh, some applauded. The man came very quickly, uttering a sharp, mouselike squeal. Jeanne's legs fell back into place.

A heavy silence filled the smoky room. Slowly Jeanne sat up, her face smeared with tears and smudged makeup. She swept the crowd with a haughty look, pulled down her skirt, and, rising to her feet, said in a firm and scornful tone:

"Let's go, gentlemen, on with the game."

She sat down again. Again she lost. This time it was a man with an extraordinarily wrinkled face and a rotting mouth who drew her toward him. He forced her to kneel before him and take between her lips a limp, repugnant-looking penis. Holding Jeanne's head between his calloused hands, he took a long time coming despite the urging of his comrades. When he climaxed at last, an almost senseless Jeanne, her face spattered with semen, fell backward in a swoon. The peach-flavored drink, poured between her lips, revived her. Kneeling by her side, Lotus made her swallow every drop if it.

"You musn't show your disgust so openly. These men are easily offended. They could take your revulsion very badly."

Very pale, her features drawn, Jeanne rose to her feet by leaning on the table. The men never took their eyes off her, yet showed no trace of impatience. They knew they would bend to their desires this beautiful stranger who looked upon them with scorn. Most of them were simple men: fishermen, unskilled laborers, water carriers. Living in the darkness of minds blunted by hard labor, they had been offered a rare treat: a beautiful woman and money with which to gamble.

The game started once more. She won a great deal a few more times, then lost again. A big man, his face covered with scars, plucked her off her seat, throwing her face down upon the table. A glass of beer spilled into her hair. She cried out as the man sodomized her for a long while.

Wild laughter broke out in the room.

This time, when Jeanne rose from her supine position there was a spot of blood upon her white suit, now nothing but a rag torn in many places. The game went on. Jeanne was winning again, then losing. She felt as though she were floating above the ground. Her bruised belly and mauled breasts felt as though they belonged to another, a stranger. Her body was no longer her own. It led an independent existence. She observed herself living, struggling. Better still: she was her own voyeur. All of a sudden she felt a brutal, savage, boundless pleasure fill every corner of her being. Hundreds of hands were caressing her, clawing at her, mercilessly exploring every part of her. Phalluses entered her, raping her lips, her belly, and her loins. She was opened, offered to each and every one. The pleasure she experienced was as mental as it was physical. Gradually, its intensity was so great that it turned to pain. She heard herself shout a last time, then sank into a reddish fog.

∞

When Lotus entered her bedchamber, it must have been a little after three in the afternoon. She opened the curtains. A warm October light flooded the room.

Jeanne stirred, shielded her eyes with her forearm. Lotus sat down on her bed.

"Did you sleep well?"

Jeanne stretched, whispering a languid yes. She smiled at Lotus, then, all of a sudden her smile changed into a grimace of pure rage. She clutched the Chinese girl by the throat. "You bitch . . . slut!"

Lotus shook herself free of this stranglehold and with her lithe grace gained the upper hand. "You didn't always hate what happened yesterday . . ."

Jeanne felt herself blush. She tried to extricate herself from Lotus's firm grip, but despite her small size the Chinese girl was the stronger one. She stopped struggling and burst out laughing. Lotus echoed her giggle.

"I wish you could have seen the boss's face at the sight of all the money you made last night. Here, just see!"

She picked up from the rug a large, white, leather briefcase bursting at the seams with bank notes and emptied it over Jeanne's head. For a while they had fun tossing the bills above the bed, setting them flying through the room. Soon, however, the two women fell back on the bed, their eyes aglow. Jeanne drew the young girl to her, unfastening the hooks on her slit Chinese dress.

"Why did you do that?"

"You were so beautiful last night."

Lotus's delicate body with its tiny breasts shone darkly next to Jeanne's pale opulence.

⌒

Jeanne was waiting in Truong's office for the Chinaman to review and sign the contracts she had brought.

"Everything is fine. . . . You'll tell Mr. George that I'm very pleased with him, and that I congratulate him for having friends such as you."

"George is not a friend, merely an acquaintance."

"An acquaintance who offered me the great pleasure of knowing you."

"And now, what do you expect from me?"

"Now you're going back to France after a stay which I hope proved pleasant for you."

"Is that all?"

"All? . . . It's immense. Without being aware of it you have given me great pleasure. I was on board ship and saw you gamble. . . . It was very beautiful, very moving. . . . I played with you a long time."

Jeanne rose, pale with anger and humiliation.

"You . . ."

"Don't say anything. Don't spoil the magnificent memory I have of you. Nothing can erase what has been. . . . And besides, I am certain that deep inside of you you do not regret that night."

Jeanne lowered her head, knowing he was right.

"To thank you, and in remembrance of your brief stay, I thought of a small present that might please you . . ." He handed her a carefully wrapped package. She was about to open it when he said, "Please, not now!"

Comfortably ensconced in her first-class seat, Jeanne watched Asia recede as she sipped a glass of champagne. As upon arrival, the customs formalities had been "eased." Truong's package, lying on the seat next to her, had not been opened. No longer able to resist her curiosity, Jeanne broke the wrapping. A beautiful lacquer box inlaid with mother-of-pearl and ivory appeared.

She opened it. Inside the black satin–lined jewel case rested the jade *olisbos*. She picked it up, examining it with admiration under the slightly shocked eye of the airline hostess. There was a small card under the precious object. She turned it over and burst out laughing as she read: "Made in Hong Kong."

The Broom Closet

*W*ith a disturbing insistence, the boy was staring at her legs, crossed under the desk. She no longer dared make a move, feeling that he was watching for the least movement that would allow him a glimpse of the inner side of her thighs. She cursed the new fashion, which, once again, had shortened women's skirts. It just so happened that this time she was not wearing slacks, having given in to the request of her new lover, philosophy teacher at the Lycée Louis-le-Grand. If only she had slipped into panty hose. But no, still to please him, she was wearing the ridiculous black garter belt that she normally wore only to spice up their sexual frolics. And that wasn't all! She wasn't even wearing panties. She was sure now that the damned brat had guessed it when, forgetting her mode of undress, she had placed a foot on her chair as she often did when she reported on the students' grades. The kid had a way of staring at her that gave her goosebumps.

Since the start of the school year, she had not paid much attention to this silently gloomy boy who, from the start, had grabbed a seat in the front row. An average student, without any special gifts or problems, he listened to the course lectures with a kind of indifference she considered affected. He was a rather good-looking adolescent, thirteen or fourteen years old, with curly brown hair, mostly untouched by comb or brush, and deep dark eyes whose serious intensity amazed in a round face, its features still submerged in childhood vagueness. Average in size, moving with a kind of lazy languor, dressed like all his pals in jeans, T-shirt, and a windbreaker, he looked like all the boys of his generation. However, having intercepted his look, she felt all of a sudden completely naked in her classroom. She blushed as she had not done in years. What a bloody little fool! she thought. Hasn't he seen a woman before? Somewhat peeved, she uncrossed her legs, then abruptly brought them close together.

He's getting on my nerves. I'm going to kick him out. Can't wait for the period to end. Another quarter of an hour. But, what is he doing? He's got his hands under the desk. He's jerking off . . . I'm sure he is . . . some nerve to do this in class, in front of all his classmates!

"Trémollet, hand me your notes!"

Ah, she was going to have a good laugh watching him pull himself together! He rose without showing the least bit of embarrassment. His clothing was perfectly in place. Silent, unfazed, he brought his homework with nimble grace over to her desk, moving smoothly in his well-worn sneakers.

"You haven't written anything. Why?"

"I didn't understand the lesson."

"Why didn't you say so? Stay after the hour. I'll go over it with you."

What had gotten into her to say this? She must have lost her mind! What an idea to remain alone with a sex-crazed boy! But you're the sex-crazed one, you silly goose! she scolded herself. Why did you ever imagine he was jerking off? It's the same as your thighs—he doesn't give a damn about your thighs.

Relieved, she deliberately spread out her legs while pretending to be totally engrossed by her reading. She thought she heard the boy swallow hard, felt his eyes exploring the secret places between her thighs, fastening on her clitoris, then plunging deep into her belly. Eyes shut, her mouth half open, her breasts taut with desire, she was filled with an almost insane urge to make love. She opened her eyes. I'm a slut! What business do I have to provoke this poor child? Sooner or later the other kids will catch on to what's going on . . .

However, the class drew to a close without incident. Amid the usual hullabaloo, the students put their things away and proceeded to leave grunting and shoving. Trémollet remained quietly in his seat. The sudden silence that enveloped the classroom brought a measure of lucidity to her mind for a moment, but then the violent eruption of desire swept away all thoughts of caution. She took a seat at the very back of the class.

"Come sit with me, Trémollet! Bring your book and notebooks." With the same lazy languor the boy made his way to her, settling next to his young math teacher.

"What don't you understand, dear boy?"

"This." He placed his hand on the young woman's thigh.

"This!" she repeated with a catch in her throat. She took the boy's hand with its bitten nails and guided it under her skirt. Together, their two hands reached the soft skin above the line of her stocking. The boy's fingers dug in.

"Stop, you're hurting me!"

The fingers continued their exploration, reaching the humid fleece.

Then, "Why did you stop?" she asked.

"We can't stay here. They're going to come soon to clean up."

"That's right. I forgot. . . . Where d'you want to go?"

"Come, I know a quiet corner." He lifted his fingers, smeared with the smell of woman, up to his nostrils: "I love it. . . . It smells good."

What a precocious boy, she reflected. She gathered the notebooks on her desk, shoving them into the market bag she used as a briefcase, and, pulling the door shut, followed Trémollet.

The boy seemed to know the old lycée from top to bottom. He walked up, down, right, left, across a courtyard, from the kitchen to the dining hall. At last he stopped in front of a door and said breathlessly to his teacher, pushing the door open: "It's here!"

A smell of stagnant water, rotting rags, engine oil, wet chalk, dirty feet, disinfectant, and bleach assailed her senses.

"What's this place? It's revolting . . ."

"We're quite safe here until tomorrow morning. It's the broom closet of the boarders' commons."

"It may be quiet, but it stinks."

"One gets used to it, you'll see," said he, pushing her firmly into the closet and closing the door behind them.

Inside it was pitch dark. At once, the boy's body glued itself to her. Annoyed, she pushed him back.

"You're not going to leave us in utter darkness, are you? Put the light on!"

"There's no light, but the other day I saw candles here, on a shelf. . . . Do you have matches?"

She rummaged through her handbag and found a lighter. The flickering flame allowed them to cast a look at the closet's contents. The boy quite easily found two candles left over from a bundle. Lighting one of them, he dripped hot wax on the corner of a shelf to hold it.

Lack of air combined with sour, stale smells nauseated the young woman, awakening memories she had assumed were buried forever. When she was five or six, she had been sent to convent school in Nancy. One of her teachers, Mlle. Jeanne, was particularly repulsive. An ageless frump of an old maid, she wore thick, woolen, gray stockings, corkscrew-twisted round her matchstick-thin legs. She was shod in shapeless black flats. Her sparse, oily hair was pulled into a bun atop her head. Her skin was lifelessly dull, covered with pimples and blackheads; her thin lips were pinched by her equine teeth. As to her eyes, black and close together, they reflected a kind of absolute spitefulness. That was Mlle. Jeanne. She hated children, particularly good-looking, well-dressed ones. She never stopped devising punishments and was happy only when her victims were reduced to tears. In her years of teaching she had become past mistress of school sadism. And, as had all the school's pretty girls, this woman, the teacher of mathematics, had had her ration of cruelly twisted pinches, pulled hair, raps on knuckles and calves with a ruler, bare-ass spankings, prolonged kneelings in the corner of the classroom or under the teacher's desk, hemmed in by gray legs stretching or retracting, liberating with every move the sour smells hidden under the old maid's ankle-length skirts and slips. But the supreme punishment was the broom closet. You were locked in there only for having committed a grievous wrong: ink blots on the homework, an insolent answer, wee-weeing in the panties, and other such transgressions. All the schoolchildren lived in dread of the broom closet. They were willing to endure the worst punishments, such as the bare-ass spanking and the enclosed space under Mlle. Jeanne's desk, rather than the closet, which contained all manner of spineless, moist, flabby beings that sprang into your face the moment you were pushed in, and others, posing as brooms, brushes, feather dusters who, in actual fact, were dragons and devils in disguise—the Ogre and the Wolf. The threat of the closet alone brought certain children to the edge of fainting or hysterics. Other victims, dragged by force despite their cries, tears, and kicks, issued later deathly pale, nostrils pinched, and lips foaming, an insane look in their eyes. Their fear was so great that none ever revealed to loving relatives the hardships endured, for fear that the Ogre and the Wolf would devour them. The most lackadaisical parents wondered at the nightmares that awakened their children, their fear of the dark. Some went so far as to consult a pediatrician.

The math teacher had been a frequent prisoner of the broom closet.

Today she had been locked in there not by Mlle. Jeanne, but by one of her students. He, however, was busy fixing up the back of the closet.

"Here, like this it'll be more comfortable."

She had but one step to take to find herself sitting on burlap bags smelling of potatoes. Trémollet urged her to lie down. She did so with the absolute repugnance she recalled from her childhood, the paralyzing terror experienced when she was five years old. She took shallow breaths of air as she had then, in order to protect herself from bad odors, but could not help but utter a small cry as her bare arm came in contact with damp sacking. Her heart was beating faster. The animals were there in the trembling light of the candle; so were the devils and dragons, the Ogre and the Wolf of her childhood. She pressed the boy's head against her belly, closed her eyes, and stammered in the imploring voice of a little girl: "I won't do it again, I promise! I'll be good, I'll do anything you want! Please, please let me go! I'm frightened. . . . I'd like to leave. Not the wolf, please. He's going to eat me, devour me! I'm afraid of his big teeth, his big tongue! No, no, not the Ogre with his sharp knife! He's going to split my belly. Oh, I'm so frightened! Mademoiselle . . . his hands grab me, undress me. . . . Not my panties, I don't have panties. . . . I wet them with my wee-wee, and Mademoiselle placed them on my head before the whole class. . . . Nana was laughing so hard she peed in her panties. . . . He's eating me, Mademoiselle, devouring my belly. What will my mummy say when she finds out that her little girl was eaten . . ."

Trémollet knelt between his teacher's legs, wiping her face with the back of his hand. She was weird, his teacher, playing at being a little girl. It was hot in the closet. He'd feel more comfortable in the buff. Without paying attention to the woman lying there, skirt raised high, blouse unbuttoned, thighs spread open, moaning and turning her head from right to left, he began to strip. She became aware of his presence and nakedness when he lay down upon her, pinning her to the ground the moment she tried to push him off.

"Please be nice, Madame, it's my first time. I never made love before . . ."

This admission brought her back to reality, dispelling the ghosts of the broom closet. She also felt as though she was about to make love for the first time. It happened to her in the summer. She was the same age as this boy, spending her summer vacation in a village, with one of her father's aunts. The house was large and cool, smelling of wax and apples. There was the neighbors' slightly retarded son. She enjoyed locking herself up with him in the attic, the cellars, the various sheds. He followed her everywhere she went, in total adoration. He would do anything she wanted: pilfer fruit from neighboring orchards, steal candy from the village grocery-tobacconist-café. She rode for hours on his shoulders. One day, a heavy storm drove them to take shelter in a small house used for storing old tools: the grindstone to sharpen scythes; cauldrons to mix the pigs' mash; old broken bicycles, their tires flat beyond repair; coal and wheelbarrows; defunct washing machines. All of a sudden she said to the boy: "Undress!" He shook his head: "No, that's naughty!" She laughed at him, calling him a dimwit, a real jerk (as she had heard the older men calling him).

"If that's the way you want it, I won't play with you anymore. I won't let you carry me. I won't kiss you anymore! Go!"

Poor Jacquot—that was his name—started to cry.

"Oh no, Olga, don't do that. I'll fetch you wild strawberries from the forest. . . . I know a good place. I'll make furniture for your doll . . ."

"I don't give a damn. Undress!"

Jacquot gave in.

Olga walked around the boy standing in the middle of the earthen floor, head down, his arms dangling, his face wet with tears, his clothing lying at his feet. One couldn't see much in the dim, stormy light filtering through a dormer window.

"You look more stupid than usual like this. Take off your sandals, and step out of your trousers!"

He followed her orders, folding in two his tall, thin body. The girl was gently hitting her friend's testicles with the tip of her espadrille. He roared: "That's wrong. You musn't touch this."

A strange phenomenon occurred then: the funny, soft tube hanging between his legs started to swell under Olga's inquisitive eye, and Jacquot's puzzled stare.

"You've got a funny thing there, like my aunt's dog, and the mayor's horse. . . . Does it hurt?" she asked, taking the raised phallus in her hand.

He shook his head no, watching his friend's small hand come and go. As she slowed down, he touched her hand.

"Don't stop, I like it, it's so good . . ."

Strangely thrilled, and feeling a slight ache, a kind of heaviness in the pit of her belly, the girl squeezed the rigid phallus.

"May I kiss it?"

No sooner said than done. She felt upon her cheek a softness she did not recognize. When she stepped back, she wiped her hands and face with the hem of her pink cotton dress, while

Jacquot contemplated with distress his shrinking organ, regaining its original dimension. They played often at this game before the end of the summer holidays, and even invented a new one.

That's the one Trémollet wanted to try. It seemed entirely normal to him. When they ran out of all the variations known to Olga, the burned-up candle went out.

Old Man Renaud's Funeral

On a splendid late morning in July, a hearse, covered with wreaths and flower bouquets, followed by a black-clad crowd, made its way through the lush countryside, accompanied by the singing of the birds, the scraping sound of heavy shoes upon the road's gravel, and the talking of the people in the procession.

An elegant young blond woman was first in line behind the hearse. She was dressed in deep mourning. Her delicate pumps were getting covered in the fine white dust of the road. A fat, red-faced man followed close behind, his black suit girded by the traditional tricolor sash. He kept on wiping his brow with a checkered cloth the size of a small towel. Behind him came the men of the village, wearing wide-brimmed, black felt hats. Among them was a very handsome, bare-headed young man. His hair was rather long and wavy. He wore a handsomely tailored, light gray suit. Then came the women, wearing straw hats or head scarves.

"That's the Martine girl up front, the dead man's granddaughter . . . hasn't been back here for years."

"What d'you suppose she'll do with old man Renaud's farm?"

"Looks like one hell of a bitch! . . ."

"Take a look at that ass. The mayor's got his nose upon it."

"And did you see the lad she brought with her? Hasn't used his hands much, that one!"

"Depends for what kind of business . . ."

"Looks just like a gal, this lad . . ."

As to the mayor, his eyes glued upon the Martine girl's stirringly ample hips, as noted by his underlings, he seemed to be on the verge of apoplexy. He loosened the knot of his tie, wiping his sweaty face and neck. At last the procession reached the cemetery, high above the village. The noonday heat intensified the heady odor of cypress. Stirred by the hearse's arrival, a flock of squawking chickens ran off in all directions.

The vehicle entered the enclosure, passing a monument to the dead. It came to a halt by an open grave at the end of the main drive. Leaning on the handle of his shovel, a grave digger, his head covered by a scraggly straw hat scorned even by scarecrows, was waiting for them. The undertaker's assistants pulled out the coffin. The car went into reverse. Following the other members of the procession, Martine, helped by the mayor, climbed atop a tombstone to let it through. The crowd, as though glued together, stood on the edge of the gaping hole. The coffin slid smoothly into the freshly dug grave.

The mayor, increasingly apoplectic and sweaty, prepared to deliver his speech. He pulled out from his pocket some folded sheets of paper covered with notes, spread them open, put on his reading glasses, and intoned in a strong voice:

"A farmer, a man of this land, this earth, Michel Renaud personified better than anyone our proud and wonderful republican traditions. Faithful to all forms of government, he stood nevertheless courageously at a distance from them all, from all commitments in fact during the difficult period of the war and occupation. This prudent avoidance of the controversies that divided our fatherland was not understood by each and every one, but it assured the esteem of our region's elite . . ."

A voice was raised in protest: "You've got to be joking! A damned collaborator is what he was . . ."

"In fact, the Free French were going to throw him into his well!"

"Don't get carried away! The Resistance movement acquired a large membership only when it was all over . . ."

"That's for sure. The deceased claimed he was one of them, because one night there was a major parachute drop in his field, right behind his farm . . ."

"Actually, it was all an error. They were supposed to land in another village. Could have been a hell of a lot of trouble for us!"

"All the same . . . the scoundrel got good and fat on the black market."

"Stop it! Quiet! Aren't you ashamed to speak ill of the dead . . . not even buried yet!"

"Quite right, Antonine. What about all of us here?"

"Better listen to our mayor. He talks good sense!"

". . . our friend, blameless morals!"

"He's taking us for dimwits, our mayor! Blameless morals . . . my eye! What about Lucette, and Marie, and the one he knocked up, fat Germaine! What about Claire, who had to leave on the quiet. And that's not counting his mistress in Bellac, and the whores in Limoges . . ."

". . . generous. . . . He gave freely to the orphanage . . ."

"Sure, he had a yen for those orphans, the little girls . . ."

"The nicest thing about him was his love of pretty girls!"

"Just like the mayor!"

"Shut up! I want to hear the end!"

". . . town councillor . . . watchful, a virtuous, simple man, a faithful friend, Michel Renaud, farewell!"

A sigh was heaved by all. Was it relief . . . or perhaps emotion?

All through the mayor's speech the beautiful mourner was trying to stifle fits of laughter within the folds of her black veil.

Approaching the open grave, the priest recited a short prayer, then sprinkled the coffin with holy water. This done, he shook hands with the girl before going over to join the group of village women. It was the girl's turn to approach the open grave. Taking the aspergillum offered her by one of the choirboys, she traced in the air what was vaguely the sign of the cross. In turn, the mayor blessed his old friend's mortal remains. Then, taking Martine's arm, he let his sweaty, shiny face brush against her black veil.

"He was a good man, your grandfather, Mademoiselle Martine, honest and virtuous."

"Not like you, Monsieur Jean."

"Why do you call me by this name? My name is Victor."

"Isn't that what they call you in Paris, at La Fiesta?"

"You're mad. Shut up!"

Monsieur Jean, or Monsieur Victor, took her aside.

"Look, the mayor's going to get laid at siesta time."

"What an old swine!"

"And the girl . . . a hell of a slut . . . right before her grandfather's open grave!"

"Come on, my girl, old man Renaud wouldn't have minded that . . . not a bit!"

"You bet your ass! The old fart must be having a hard-on in his coffin."

One by one, the mourners expressed their deepest sympathy to Martine, and to the mayor standing by her side, still puzzled.

"God damn it, who are you?" the mayor muttered.

The priest heard that, and cast a reproachful look in the direction of the mayor, who shrugged his shoulders by way of an apology. Instead of answering, Martine lifted her veil.

"Clara! That's a good one! Who'd expect . . . the granddaughter of that swine Renaud! Good blood never lies! One of Paris's greatest tarts. . . . You won't breathe a word, will you?"

"Perhaps not, if you swear the same, Monsieur le maire . . ."

"Shake on it! All in all, I'm rather glad to see you! We'll have a good laugh or two! Who's the kid you brought along?"

"My lover."

"Your lover?"

Victor burst out laughing under the shocked looks of the village women. The guffaw ended in an embarrassed gurgling.

"Forgive me . . . the heat . . . nervousness . . ."

Martine's arm began to ache from being shaken by so many rough, callous hands. Her throat was dry from the many thanks she uttered with each handshake. Phew, she thought, here comes the last one!

"Dominick, I can't take it anymore."

She threw herself into the embrace of the young man in the gray suit.

"Monsieur le maire, I wish to present to you Dominick. You've met him before."

"Good morning, Monsieur Jean."

The two young people could hardly contain their laughter before the mayor's astonished expression.

"But I don't know this gentleman!"

"Oh, yes, you know him! But it doesn't matter. Dominick will be as discreet as I am. Isn't this so, Dominick?"

"Of course, my angel! Aren't we among people of our class?"

Martine and Dominick walked away, an arm round each other's waist. They were followed by the perplexed, frowning mayor, who couldn't stop wiping his brow.

As he walked, Dominick kept on pecking Martine's neck.

"D'you realize you're particularly exciting in your widow's weeds? You turn me on. I want you."

"Stop. We're going to shock them! First of all, I'm hungry."

"Me, too! And how!"

A breathless mayor caught up to them.

"As for myself, I'm ravenous. I could swallow an ox. Dame Poulard has prepared a wonderful lunch. Old man Renaud left all kinds of instructions as to this last meal. He used to say it would be a polite, formal farewell addressed to those who'd known him, and that, on a full stomach, their tongues might lose their sharpness. He was a bon vivant, that one!"

Having uttered what he believed to be a witticism, the mayor broke into a good-natured laugh, which caused some country women, who had lingered on the side of the road, to turn round.

∞

In the spacious common hall of old man Renaud's farm, women, their bellies girded by wide aprons, were bustling about, setting long tables whose thick, white tablecloths suggested generations of trousseau makers. These women borrowed from close neighbors the additional tableware necessary for such a large number of guests. Because of the disparate combinations of plates and platters from various households, the tables acquired the festive character of an improvised picnic. Leafy shoots strewn with rose petals meandered in between the settings. Garlands wrought from old, illustrated newspapers found in the attic covered the freshly whitewashed walls. They spiraled round last year's post office almanac, made from a piece of bark on which an artist had painted the Mont-Saint-Michel gleaming under a sunset of tarnished spangles. They circled a chromolithograph of a girl holding a spray of flowers, and the portraits of old man Renaud's parents. A tool rack—in which the farmer had stored some dozen old pipes, each more seasoned than the next, with some definitely out of use; a crucifix encrusted with flyspecks; and two plates, one showing a blue boat, the other a green castle—was prominently displayed. The cuckoo clock, which never struck on time despite frequent trips to the old clockmaker of Limoges's rue des Arènes, was inhabited by a bird whose conduct was highly unpredictable. It came cuckooing out far more frequently than necessary. Irritated by the yearly visits of this insurgent mechanism, the clockmaker suggested one day that old man Renaud would do well to acquire a more modern timepiece. Wildly furious, the old man snatched his cuckoo clock, together with his patronage, from the artisan's hands, calling him a useless bungler bringing his clients to utter ruin. Since that incident, the capricious cuckoo had struck the hours at his own rhythm. As Renaud used to say, "He must have his own reasons."

Above the high fireplace a picture of the deceased, wearing the Zouave uniform, reigned supreme. The vividly colored photograph was truly impressive. Of course, there was no one around who recalled seeing Michel Renaud wearing his military service uniform. There were no draftees of his class left.

From the cooking ranges rose rich and generous odors. The first guests were starting to arrive.

The large room was full when Martine came down from the second floor, where she had removed her black veil and somber dress. She was now wearing a light black and white silk dress, with a V-neck décolleté plunging between her breasts. She trailed a strong scent of Shalimar. Dominick followed close by, still impeccable in his gray suit. The mayor was playing the role of master of ceremonies, placing the special guests of the deceased at the table. Martine was given the seat of honor, with the priest to her right, and on her left the man she called Monsieur Jean. Dominick was squeezed between two sprightly plump women. The waitresses began to ladle out a vermicelli chicken broth from huge soup tureens. This course was followed by all manner of local hams, sausages, and pâtés, and a chanterelle omelette. At first the only sounds were the clickety-click of forks and knives, the flowing of wine poured into clinking glasses, and masticating jaws. Everyone poured wine into his soup except for the vaguely nauseated Martine and Dominick. When the poultry was brought in, shirt sleeves were rolled up, ties removed, belts loosened, blouses unbuttoned. A thick, almost black, red wine, drawn from the cool cellar's barrels, flowed abundantly, staining chins and tablecloths. When the leg of lamb arrived with its white beans, string beans cleaned of every bit of string, everybody was flushed, glistening with perspiration, slovenly, and giggly. Even the priest found it hard to maintain his dignity. As to the mayor, his hand was hard at work under the table. Martine, her eyes half closed, her body lolling back in her chair, wore a beatific smile. As to Dominick, his hands full of his table mates' ample charms, he was not inactive. The green salad and cheeses were served amid the hubbub of a wedding feast rather than that of a wake.

The priest was the first to throw his hand in. He staggered from the table to a linden tree in front of the house, and promptly collapsed. His departure was hailed, unleashing lewd gestures repressed until then. The men drew the farm girls down to sit in their laps. A couple of men at a time crowded around one or another of the servants, opening her bodice, or feeling her up under her skirt. The girls, young and fresh, made a show of struggling, laughing and squealing, but their eyes shone brightly, as they pushed the men away halfheartedly, their slow motion giving the lie to their words. Those servants who succeeded in breaking free from daring hands brought in bowls overflowing with chocolate mousse, and cream custard to be poured over cherry trifle, staining lips and fingers. When coffee and liqueurs were finally brought in, the older men and women withdrew, assuming dignified airs; then, after pissing all along the stable wall, they collapsed under the linden tree where the priest had been the first to claim his spot. Sonorous snores echoed through the sudden void.

The vast hall smelled like a lair, exhaling the mingled odors of spilled wine, roast, chocolate, tobacco, sweaty armpits, stale wood fire, and racing stable. A table that had given way under the weight of a couple far too inebriated to carry out their amorous intent was nothing but a pile of planks scattered upon the uneven stony pavement. The man, despite his own efforts and the eager assistance of his companion, could not rise to his feet. Unbuttoned, fly wide open, he had fallen upon his back, legs spread apart—fat obscene animal—lying upon a formerly sparkling white tablecloth now stained by the wreckage of the meal. His snores signified only too plainly to the disappointed female the necessity of seeking gratification elsewhere. She noticed a tall, foolish-looking fellow whose randy look was taking in this scene, while with his hand deep in his trouser pocket he stroked his erect member, and lost no time in speaking up:

"C'mon, Lucien, is this how you carry on in the presence of ladies?"

Lucien neighed rather than laughed, speeding up his stroking with a satisfied air.

"Stop, you bad boy . . . stop wasting good stuff! Let's go to the stable. They've just changed the horses' straw. Animal smells turn me on."

Tearing his hand out of his pocket, she dragged him in the direction of the stable, lurching like a boat on the high seas.

A chubby-faced servant girl, whose large breasts popped out of her loosened blouse, exuded a pungent odor from the curly fleece of her armpits. She was laughingly beating off the attack of two strong fellows in shirt sleeves who were trying to force her down upon one of the tables. They had their way, with the girl landing flat on her stomach, her nose in a plate still full of chocolate mousse, which she spread joyfully all over her face. One of the two fellows pushed up her skirt. What appeared then was a magnificent ass, huge, firm, white as ivory, split in two by a high, dark furrow emphasizing its gleaming whiteness.

"Good God, is that a beautiful ass! Come look, René! You've got to see it to believe it!"

"Right you are! An ass like this, you've got to go down on your knees to worship it properly!"

No sooner said than done. René spread the two buttocks apart, firmly planting a resounding kiss on one of them. His pal shoved him aside, whipping out a phallus of imposing dimensions. He brought the girl's wide hips toward him, and plunged in, uttering a woodcutter's grunt, "huh!" echoed by the girl's sigh of satisfaction. René watched with growing covetousness his friend busying himself. Overtaken by the excitement of this moving scene, he slipped under the table so as not to lose one moment of it.

Under another table, a couple lying head to foot were pleasuring each other, while in a corner a woman of mature years was sucking off a boy, who, glass in hand, watched her mouth come and go.

The mayor, apoplectically flushed, his right hand still under the table, his eyes popping out of his head, looked on the edge of a stroke as Martine opened one by one the buttons of his fly, letting her delicate fingers slip into the slit of his trunks.

"Stop, girlie! Let's go to the barn . . . we'll be nice and private!"

"Why bother? It's very nice right here!"

"But I want you naked. . . . Stop! You're making me come!"

"And isn't that what you want, Monsieur Jean!"

"Don't call me that here. We're not in Paris!"

"That's right, we're not in Paris, but it's just as bad in your stink hole!"

"You don't mind a bit, you slut!"

Martine moaned, opening herself to the mayor's fingers, while he, slumped upon his chair, let out a roar.

"Oh, no! Didn't I tell you to stop?"

"Never mind, we'll have another go next time, old boy!"

During this whole time, Dominick had valiantly resisted the assaults on his person of his two alluring table companions, who, taken together, must have weighed five hundred pounds. Finally, he was forced to flee the jeering, disappointed damsels.

"That boy's got nothing in his pants! . . ."

"Go on, you drip. No balls there!"

"Some man! That's a girl, yes sir!"

"Look at Victor over there! He's not wasting his time."

"That ain't fair!"

The two girls staggered in the direction of the mayor, who, having pulled himself together, was urging Martine to follow him.

"Come to the barn. Appetizers stir my juices."

"Not now. I'm going to join Dominick."

"Hey, Victor! Anything wrong with us? . . . You weren't putting on airs last time."

"Right you are, you big humps. Great to tear off a piece of ass with old friends. Let's go to it, the three of us together, like always."

The three of them could hardly make it through the door, however. Finally, they squeezed through, arms round one another's waists. Off they went, howling bawdy songs at the top of their lungs.

No sooner had they left than Dominick's head appeared at a wide-open window, framed by geranium pots.

"Psst! You're alone at last! About time, too!"

Lithe as a cat, he stepped over the windowsill, almost landing on a fat man sound asleep on the ground. Martine put her arms around Dominick's neck, kissing him tenderly.

"They're a scream, the people of your village. Are they always like this?"

"Only on holidays: baptisms, communions, weddings, funerals, the annual fair, and long ago at vintage season and harvesting. On other days they're not a bit funny. That's why I left the place. Can you see me taking care of my kids and pigs? Come, I'll show you my hiding place."

She pulled him in the direction of a flight of stairs. Both ran up. Through a half-open door they heard moans and the rhythmic creaking of springs. Deeply stirred, Martine rubbed herself against Dominick, who pushed her against the wall, pulling up her skirt.

"Not here . . . come!"

They went up a steeper flight of stairs. Martine pushed open a decrepit old door, and they found themselves in a vast granary partly filled with wheat. Martine threw herself face down on the surprisingly fresh seeds. She poured them along her breasts and her arms, laughing like a little girl. Dominick was looking at her tenderly. Martine got up and opened a trap door. The stubbornly sweet odor of hay rose up, connected with memories of happy holidays. She sat down, her legs swinging over the opening. Then she let herself fall, followed at once by Dominick. They remained motionless for a while, adjusting their sight to the semidarkness. Three of the wooden walls were made of worm-eaten planks, and in the interstices between them one could see thin rays of golden light containing dancing particles of dust.

"When I was little, I often hid here to play with the local boys. We had to hide because Granddad did not like the idea of our playing in the attic. He always feared we were up to no good."

"Must have been so!"

"Not really, unless playing doctor, or husband and wife, should be considered naughty!"

"Show me how you play doctor . . ."

In this familiar place that reminded her of her childhood, Martine, her hair full of hay, looked like a little girl. She was much more moving in this guise than as the sophisticated young woman used to certain Paris nightclubs such as Elle et Lui, the Katmandou, and the ever-unchanging Moune.

Dominick took off his jacket and shoes, opened the zipper of his trousers.

"Wait, let me do it!"

Martine took hold of the two legs of the trousers and pulled them off so swiftly that she fell back with her skirt covering her head. A skip and a jump brought her back, and she removed her thin black stockings. Crawling in the hay, she lay down upon her friend, biting playfully his neck and ears.

"Stop, you're tickling me! Stop . . . stop! You'll see where this gets you . . ."

He toppled her over, holding her firmly under him by her wrists.

"Take off my dress!" ordered Martine, her voice gone suddenly husky.

The light dress slipped off, as in a dream, revealing Martine's body, totally nude.

"How beautiful you are!"

Dominick's hands caressed the lovely form covered with a thin veil of perspiration. Soon it seemed tattooed with yellow, blue, and white petals and faded green leaves. Martine tore off rather than removed Dominick's shirt.

Nothing lovelier than these two bodies: the slender golden one of the blond Martine, with its heavy, firm, round breasts, and the slightly tanned one of Dominique, lithe with its incredibly slender waist, which brought out the roundness of her hips, and the pertness of two small breasts with their wide, dark areolas.

The two girls slid toward each other in one graceful movement, slow and silky.

Outside, the heat of the day had finally cooled. Old man Renaud's guests were asleep, a sated smile upon their lips.

The deceased would have been pleased: so far as funerals go, it had been a really fine one.

The Truck Driver

"*T*here you go . . . fine! Don't move now. . . . Side view now. . . . Hold your dress as though you wanted to raise it. Not quite so high . . . good! Look at me. . . . Lower your head . . . not so much! Perfect! Don't move now! One more . . ."

"Hurry, I'm a bit tired."

"Artists need more time, my dear."

"Some artist! Underpaid, dead broke, owes me plenty of bread."

"Come on, be nice! It'll be over soon. At the end of this week you'll get paid. Promise!"

Nathalie burst out laughing: Aldo's money! No catching sight of it this week, that's for sure! However, it didn't matter. She was one of the best-paid models in Italy. Besides, Aldo was an old pal who knew her when she was a waif, with holes in her socks and dresses barely covering her small buttocks. It'd be a sad day indeed if one couldn't help out a friend. The ring of the telephone made her jump. Cursing all the way, Aldo walked over to pick it up. "Shit, people don't let you work! Hello? Who? Nathalie? Yes, she's here! She's coming! It's for you. . . . Get a move on. I've got other things to do."

Nathalie took the receiver from him. "Oh shit! Hello, it's you. . . . Good morning . . ."

She perched on a corner of the table crowded with photos, which she looked through absentmindedly. "Why not? When? Next week? Perhaps . . . It might be fun. So long." She hung up looking pensive.

"Stop woolgathering. Back to work!"

"OK, let's go!"

She resumed her pose, but a more languid, more sensuous one. Aldo cheered her on.

"You see, when you're with it, things begin to roll."

She smiled, whispering to herself, "A truck driver . . ."

∞

Traveling in the direction of Rome along an expressway, two drivers of a twenty-ton truck—Paolo, a very good-looking, wide-shouldered, and tender-eyed boy, and Giuseppe, a typical womanizing braggart—were singing a Neapolitan ballad at the top of their lungs.

Giuseppe reached for two cans of beer propped on the back cot, and handed one to Paolo, who promptly opened it with his teeth, making the foam spurt out. The two pals drank to the health of ladies of the night, expecting them farther on.

"To gorgeous Luciana!"

"To beautiful Mila!"

"To all the beautiful Roman babes!"

"To Italy's greatest asses!"

The truck slowed down, leaving the highway for a smaller road running through the woods. On each side of the road prostitutes awaited their clients, some seated round a wood fire, others dancing, their ears glued to their radios. A handsome brunette, Giorgina, was the first to recognize the truck.

"Hey, girls, it's Paolo, yes, Paolo!"

The heavy truck came to a stop, and the girls ran toward it shouting, "Paolo, Paolo!" They climbed up on the footboards, the fenders, the back bumper. One of them knocked on the windshield. "Hey, Paolo! You're real cute in your display window. It could be Amsterdam . . ."

Giorgina shrugged her shoulders.

"If Paolo so much as touched this thing, it'd sell at an exorbitant price."

Paolo and Giuseppe laughed, pleased with the enthusiastic reception they were getting from the girls. A small, battered Innocenti came to a stop on the opposite side of the road.

"Giorgina, that's for you!"

"That creep always gets here at the wrong moment!"

A short, fat sexagenarian, wearing a crumpled suit, summoned Giorgina with a wave of his pudgy hand.

"All right, I'm coming. . . . Wait for me, Paolo, it won't take a minute!"

She crossed the road, hips rolling, buttocks tightly held by her shorts, transistor radio swinging from her wrist.

"Hi, Giorgina! I said to myself I'd better go chat a bit with my pal Giorgina . . ."

"Look, if it's talk you're after, forget it! But to toss one off, OK."

"Oh, Giorgina, I can't stand it when you talk like that!"

Giorgina dragged him toward the thickets. The little man stumbled, almost losing his balance, which unleashed peals of laughter from the onlookers.

The other girls started dancing round the truck. Giuseppe mimed a belly dance. Paolo, from inside, clapped rhythmically. A girl, perched on a fender, glued her lips to the windshield, shouting, "Paolo, you're gorgeous like a truck!" Aroused, the other women followed suit. Soon, the whole windshield was smeared with wet lipstick marks.

Giorgina came out from the thickets, smoothing her hair, and followed by the man, who was trying to buckle his trousers.

"Giorgina, wait till I'm dressed. . . . Help me . . ."

"If it's a nurse you need, you've got the wrong party!"

"What's the matter with you today?"

"Today there's Paolo. . . . Get a move on. Ciao!"

She ran toward the truck, leaving her vexed client standing there. She climbed into the truck's cab, and snuggling up to Paolo, kissed him on both cheeks.

"I'm real glad to see you. It's been a while. Where were you?"

"With Giuseppe. We didn't stop. We were in France, Belgium, Holland."

"That's some lucky break, traveling all over like that."

"You can come with me any time you want."

"Stop, don't set me dreaming!"

A girl's head appeared at the cab's door.

"Watch out, Giorgina, here comes Marco!"

A red Lancia stopped behind the truck as the girls resumed their stations on both sides of the road. Giorgina kissed Paolo and opened the cab's door.

"So long, guy. I'm off."

Paolo held her back.

"Are you scared?"

"Not for myself. I'm used to blows. But I don't want you hurt."

"Don't you worry about me, but I'm going to say a word or two to this poor bugger."

"Drop it. If you don't, I'll get in trouble. Please don't. Do it for me!"

Paolo shrugged his shoulders.

"After all, it's your business. I'll come to see you in a few days. You're coming, Giuseppe?"

Giorgina jumped down from the truck and joined the other girls without a look at the Lancia.

The twenty-ton pursued its course. Behind it, the Lancia took off. A few kilometers later they reached the outskirts of Rome, stopping at a truckers' filling station with a blinking neon sign: CASA LUCIANA. Some fifteen trucks were parked there.

"Big crowd today at beauteous Luciana."

The Lancia stopped at the other end of the parking lot. Paolo started toward it.

"Are you kicking up a fuss, Paolo?"

"C'mon, guy, you'll take your own sweet time to piss before croaking, won't you?"

It was getting dark. The night was going to be cool. Rubbing his hands together, Paolo approached the Lancia. He quietly opened the zipper of his fly. Then, "Sorry, I didn't see you . . ."

Looking stupid, Marco, leaning against his car, peered down at his elegant patent leather boots and the bottom of his now splattered trousers. Paolo straightened out his clothing. Finally understanding what just happened, Marco, flushed with rage, took a step forward.

"Fucker! My boots . . ."

"It's nothing! They'll dry!"

"Dry? You bastard! Custom-made boots . . . brand new. Wipe them!"

"If I dirtied your boots, it's only fair I should clean them!"

Paolo took hold of the squealing pimp, plunging him into a large keg full of dirty water and then, whistling softly to himself, slowly walked in the direction of the restaurant.

When Paolo went through the door, a rush of warm air, odors, and noises assailed him.

"We knocked in five goals!"

"All sluts, all bitches, that's what they are!"

"One Chianti coming up, one!"

"*All* sluts—don't lay it on so thick. If you had only known my mamma . . ."

"How about my coffee? Is it coming?"

"Let's leave your mom out of it, but as to the others, nothing but sluts."

"Bringing in number 8 clinched the victory."

"Get a load of Mila's ass! Getting rounder every day!"

The plump brunette's buttocks received a resounding slap.

"Mr. Luigi, is that a way of behaving? Oh, Mr. Paolo!"

Paolo had just slipped his fingers into the waitress's cleft, which earned him the owner's angry look.

"Go on with your work, Mila. Our clients are in a hurry!"

"But, Madame, this is Mr. Paolo . . ."

The door opened with such a commotion that all of Luciana's clients stopped talking and eating, and turned to see Marco, a long knife in his hand dripping dirty water. He was so ridiculous and pitiful that the whole room guffawed despite the menacing weapon. Some of the truck drivers, Paolo and Giuseppe among them, walked in his direction. Seeing their number, he drew back.

"Sorry, must be a mistake. I'm looking for some friends. . . . You wouldn't have a towel?"

He looked round and found himself face to face with a colossus who lifted him with one finger and carried him outside. A huge "plouf" was heard. Paolo whispered with awe: "Two baths in one day!"

Paolo made his way to the bar, where Luciana, a well-shaped, desirable redhead, was nervously wiping glasses.

"Hi, Luciana, glad to see me?"

"I don't like it when you fart around like that!"

"Stop bitching and give me a kiss . . ."

She offered her lips from behind the counter.

"You've gotten here much too late, you and Giuseppe. Nothing left in the kitchen."

"Give it a try! I'm ravenous!"

"All right. Here's a table. Mila, get number 10 ready for Paolo and Giuseppe."

The two friends, greeted by their pals, made their way through the room to their table. Mila was right there, setting down a bottle of wine before them.

"What shall I bring you?"

"Two carbonaras."

"Properly served, as for two sick men! . . ."

They ate and drank in silence while customers were gradually filing out.

Belching, Giuseppe wiped his chin, which was stained by tomato sauce.

"Wouldn't mind tossing one off . . ."

Paolo slapped his back, laughing, and poured him another glass of wine.

"You're programmed. When you finish eating, you've got to fuck."

With the last client out the door, Luciana locked the front door and took off her apron.

"Like that we'll be nice and quiet," she said, taking a chair between Paolo and Giuseppe. Giuseppe got up and tried to catch Mila, who escaped his grasp. He caught up with her in the kitchen, pushing her down upon a long table covered by a checkered green and white oil cloth.

"Oh, Mr. Giuseppe!"

No time was being wasted in the restaurant either. Seated in Paolo's lap, a softly giggling Luciana, her breasts exposed, let her friend stroke them.

"Come, Paolo dear, let's go up to my room. We'll be more comfortable."

Paolo liked Luciana's room. He thought it was elegant with its pink satin bedspread, Pierrot doll, needlework cushions, flowered orange, pink, and green wallpaper, skirted dressing table adorned by a large ribbon matching the heavily lined draperies, colorful knickknacks, and the reproductions on the walls, particularly the one of *La Cruche cassée*, his favorite.

Despite Paolo's ardor, Luciana took the time to carefully remove and fold the delicate pink bedspread. This procedure gave Paolo time to undress. Courteously, he helped Luciana pull her dress over her head, and then he stretched out on her bed.

Paolo lighted a cigarette while Luciana watched him in her dressing-table mirror.

"How I love to make love with you!"

Paolo let escape the self-satisfied laugh of a male who is sure of himself. He reached for an old copy of *Playboy* lying on the low table by the side of the bed.

"Get a load of these chicks. Incredible!"

He let a dreamy finger follow the voluminous curves of a blond.

"I wouldn't mind paying for one like this!"

"Too expensive for you, gorgeous!"

He sat up and caught her by her arm, drawing her to him.

"Nothing is too good for a man like me. You know it, don't you? Eight days . . . if I could only have eight days with a cover girl like that."

"Eight days! Think of the number of trips you'd have to make to afford that!"

"You don't understand. Money isn't important—what counts is the dream."

"The dream, the dream—you make me laugh," said Luciana. walking away from her lover.

"Chicks don't know about dreaming. My motorcycle is still fine . . . but I could get a new one next year . . . ," he whispered to himself.

☜

In front of the Piazza di Spagna, Paolo, bundled up in a navy blue suit, hair too neatly combed, tie too tightly knotted, was pacing up and down, a bouquet wrapped in wrinkled paper in his hand. He had arrived a half hour early, worried sick over missing his appointment. But how late she was! He'd been walking about for over an hour under the mocking eyes of the peddlers on the steps. At last a taxi screeched to a stop near him. A very pretty blond stepped out, elegantly dressed in a black tailored suit with a slit skirt. Her appearance was greeted by whistles from the local skirt-chasers. She cast a knowing look around her, noticed Paolo, and smiled. With mincing steps, calculated to drive mad all males in the vicinity, she made her way toward him.

"I'm Nathalie. You're waiting for me?"

Paolo blushed deeply and stuttered, "Yes, yes. I'm the one. I mean to say . . . I was waiting for you. My name is Paolo. . . . Here, this is for you."

He handed her the flowers, drooping from too long a wait.

"Thank you. That's nice. Where are we going?"

"I don't know. Your place. Oh, I forgot!" He took a bankroll out of his pocket.

Nathalie threw him an annoyed look.

"Not here? Right, sorry. You know Rome, don't you?"

"Rather well. Where's your car?"

"My car? I've got something better than that. A motorcycle."

"A motorcycle?"

Slightly taken aback, she nevertheless followed Paolo to his superbly waxed machine. Shrugging her shoulders, she pulled up her narrow skirt, revealing pretty lace garters. Paolo straddled his machine, and turning back to his passenger, inquired:

"Where are we going?"

"To my place at the Hilton."

Immensely proud of having such a pretty girl hooked to his waist, Paolo took her for a ride through antique Rome, then headed for the suburbs. They went through a little wood where, on each side of the road, prostitutes were waiting for their clients. As they passed, Paolo waved.

"Look at that," said Giorgina. "Couldn't he have stopped a moment?"

The motorcycle went speeding past Marco's Lancia.

∞

Paolo had never set foot in such a place. He was looking at everything with an admiration he did not try to disguise. His motorcycle helmet propped under one arm, the wilting roses in the other hand, summoned a smile to the lips of the Hilton personnel, usually blasé about the attitudes, mode of dress, and verbal expression of their clients. Nathalie took her key from the concierge at the desk and went to the elevators, followed by Paolo. For him the apartment seemed a palace.

"Is this your room?"

"No, it's my suite's living room."

"Ah, your suite," repeated Paolo. He did not have a clue to what she was saying.

"Make yourself comfortable. I'll be back."

Left alone, he placed his helmet down carefully on a heavily gilded chest of drawers that impressed him no end. He produced once more his formidable roll of paper money, placing it where it could readily be seen on a small secretary, next to the roses. Satisfied with these arrangements, he sat down on the edge of a chair.

Nathalie returned wearing a black silk chiffon negligee, edged with swansdown, and carrying a bottle of champagne and two glasses.

"Shall we have a drink? Why don't you open the bottle."

Paolo picked up the bottle and showed her the bills. Opening the drawer of the secretary, she placed them carefully inside.

"You're not counting them?"

"I trust you. Now open the bottle!"

He spilled some of the champagne.

"Cheers, Paolo!"

They clinked glasses, then drank in silence.

"Come close to me. Sit down. Are you afraid of me? D'you want some music?"

Without waiting for an answer, she pressed down one of the buttons of the radio. Stravinsky's "*Sacre du printemps*" filled the room.

"D'you like this?"

Paolo made a face that left no doubt as to his tastes in music. Nathalie pressed down another button. The syrupy voice of a fashionable Italian singer replaced the Stravinsky.

"Better, isn't it?" asked Nathalie, kissing Paolo, who let her do so without the least reaction. "I don't appeal to you?"

"Oh, yes, but it's all this," he answered, his gesture indicating the surroundings. "Come, let's go to the bedroom!"

"Oh, yes, the bedroom . . ."

Seeing nothing but the bed, he rubbed his hands together like a boy. Tenderly, Nathalie took to undressing him. He took her in his arms, embraced her with renewed vigor.

"You're so beautiful. You smell so good!"

She finished undressing him.

"You're not bad, either."

She pulled him toward the bed, on which they fell laughing. Her lips moved all over Paolo's large, muscular, tanned body. He was letting her make love to him, wondering whether he was not dreaming, if indeed it was him in this silk-covered boudoir, with paintings in gilded frames on the walls, upon a bed covered with fur blankets, with a girl more beautiful than he could ever have imagined. Luciana's pink room seemed far away and ordinary. He gently pushed back Nathalie's head, lying down upon her.

∽

"Come on, it's nothing. It happens to every man occasionally."

"I don't give a damn about all men! It's the first time it ever happened to me. In every city, every country I drive through, girls remember Paolo and his truck."

"It's nothing at all. Don't let it upset you! Stay calm!"

"Stay calm? But I don't want to calm down! It's because of where we are, this place of yours. It intimidates me. It's too chic. It makes me go all limp, like a cold shower."

"We could go elsewhere if you wish. Why don't you take me to your truck?"

Paolo gave her an incredulous look.

"Really? You'd be willing to do this?"

"Yes, why not? It would be a change for me."

"All right, let's go!"

Nathalie jumped down from the bed.

"One minute and I'm ready."

Paolo jumped up, uttering a triumphant war cry. He had forgotten his fiasco. Grabbing the bottle of champagne by the neck, he took a swallow of the tepid liquid. A bit of foam ran down his chin. He was humming as he dressed. Nathalie returned wearing a tight pair of jeans, a T-shirt, and a brown leather jacket.

"Oh, no, you won't stay dressed like this! I like to put my hand—sorry, that's not what I meant to say . . ."

"But you did say it."

She went out of the room. When she returned again, she was wearing a flowing dress, buttoned down the front. Paolo exclaimed approvingly: "Fine! It's much prettier and more practical."

∞

Night was falling softly upon the Italian countryside. Inside the cab of the truck Nathalie seemed to have fallen asleep. The skirt of her dress had slipped up, revealing the top of her stockings. While driving, Paolo could not keep from casting frequent looks at these beautiful, offered thighs. With one hand, he moved the light material higher. The young woman's black garters stood out against the whiteness of her flesh. He caught sight of her lace panties. Paolo felt his penis harden, rise. He slowed down and unbuttoned the top of her dress. The truck's vibration sent a quiver through his passenger's breasts; she let out a slight moan. The heavy truck left the road, stopping on a strip of flat ground designed for temporary parking. The throbbing of the motor was followed by a deep silence. Paolo completed the unbuttoning of the dress and remained a long time in contemplation of his sleeping beauty. Lights from the cars passing on the road swept over Nathalie's nakedness, lending it the haunting character of something unreal. His lips caught the nipples of the young woman's breasts; she let out another light moan. He drew her to him, kissing her eyes, lips, neck.

"I want you."

She opened her pale blue eyes, whispering, "So do I."

In spite of the cab's narrowness, he was able to undress rapidly. He helped Nathalie stretch out upon the cot placed behind the front seats. His prick, grown hard, ached with desire. He lifted her up, gently had her straddle him, and slid right into her. He remained a long time inside her without moving, savoring his conquest at last. Then, sure of himself, he made love to her. When she cried out, leaning backward, it was his turn to be happy.

For a long time the mist that covered the windows isolated them from the rest of the world.

"I'm hungry," Nathalie said, buttoning up her dress.

"I know a place not too far from here that must still be open."

"Let's go there!"

"You know, it doesn't look a bit like your palaces."

"I couldn't care less. I'm hungry."

Humming softly, Paolo started the truck. Nathalie snuggled against him, looking at the trees going by on each side of the road. Soon, the heavy vehicle turned off onto a secondary road.

∞

Heat, odors, noises assailed them as they pushed open the restaurant door.

"Is the spaghetti coming, Mila?"

"Bring on a bottle of Chianti. It's my treat this time!"

"We knocked in three goals—three!"

"Hey, Luciana, look who's just come in . . ."

"Hey, Paolo, you're in the wrong flick, boy!"

"Hi, everybody!"

"Well, you old bugger, you don't waste any time, do you?"

"Paolo, you look bushed. Need a hand?"

Paolo walked across the room, holding Nathalie by the hand. Wiping glasses nervously behind her counter, Luciana watched them approach.

"Hello, Luciana, this is my friend Nathalie."

Without bothering to set her glass down, Luciana nodded, "Hello, miss."

"Hello, madam."

"We don't 'madam' here, she's just Luciana."

"Hello, Luciana. We're very hungry. Can we still get some dinner?"

"Go over there, to Giuseppe's table. He's Paolo's best friend. Over there, the big guy waving."

"Not bad looking, your friend. Are they all like this?"

"Almost all. Go. I'll join you."

Nathalie walked toward the table pointed out to her, followed by the looks and lewd remarks of the seated truckers.

"Stay with us, miss! This one's just as good as your guy."

"Watch out for gorgeous Luciana. The woman's a tigress!"

Giuseppe got up, hustling his pals.

"Shut up, the lot of you. Behave yourselves. There's a lady in the house. Sit down, miss. They've got big traps, but not a mean bone in their bodies, save one perhaps."

"They don't scare me," she said, settling down at his table.

Still wiping her glass, Luciana did not take her eyes off the pretty blond. Next she glanced at Paolo, who wore the self-satisfied expression of a gloating male.

"So, you're pleased with yourself. You got yourself what you wanted. Just between us, do these girls make love better than we do?"

Paolo pulled her toward him, whispering something in her ear. Luciana burst out laughing, looking at Nathalie.

"Come on, go sit down. Your beauty's waiting."

"Your friend is charming," Nathalie said, stroking Giuseppe's hand as Paolo settled down with them.

Mila set down steaming plates of spaghetti in front of them, and they dipped right in.

"So I was right, wasn't I? There's no nicer guy than Giuseppe. And tender with the ladies," Paolo mumbled, his mouth full of food.

"Stop your kidding! Paolo's a pal. We're like brothers," Giuseppe added, blushing, while under the table Nathalie's hand, then her foot, grew restless under Paolo's amused eye. He leaned toward her, asking in a half whisper, "D'you like him?"

"Yes, rather."

"I'm not jealous, you know. If you want to go with him, there's a small room up there . . ."

Giuseppe's eyes were going from one to the other. He wanted to make out whether they were joking or not.

"D'you like me?" Nathalie questioned provocatively.

"Oh, yes . . ."

"Well, come on then!"

She got up, accompanied by a triumphant-looking Giuseppe, and made her way across the room followed by the envious glances of the suddenly silent men. Midway up the stairs, she stopped, assuming a provocative pose, and addressed the crowd in a voice grown low and husky: "Follow me who will!"

With a roar the men all rose to their feet and rushed up in her wake, pushing and shoving on the narrow stairs. Soon, only Luciana and Paolo remained downstairs, tightly squeezed against one another.

"She was very beautiful. You're not sorry?"

"No, she made me understand one thing . . ."

"What's that?"

"That I've got you under my skin. Come on, let's get out of here."

They rushed out of the empty room, running toward the truck.